Inn of Three Graces

~ *a story of adventure, intrigue and comedy* ~

Carol Lazzeri ~ Cheryl Doyle

Copyright © 2017 Carol Lazzeri & Cheryl Doyle
All rights reserved.
Carol Lazzeri and Cheryl Doyle assert the moral right to be identified as the authors of this work.
The story is entirely a work of fiction..
Cover and interior illustrations by Laura LeClair.
All rights reserved.
Second Edition April 2018

ISBN:
13:9781975857219
10:1975857216
Printed in the USA by Create Space

For Autographed Copies:
Inn3Graces@aol.com
or order at
www.amazon.com/dp/1975857216
or, http://www.smile.amazon.com/ch/30-0630665
and search Inn of Three Graces
(to support North Port Coalition for Homeless/Needy Children, Inc. a/k/a Back Pack Angels)

To Back Pack Angels with love

I. The Meeting

Allie McInerney stretched out in her beach chair, open book face down on her lean belly with a wide-brimmed straw hat covering her face. The day was on the wane and a perfect way to spend a mid-fall Sunday afternoon.

The week had been hectic at her firm, requiring her to spend three days in Seattle on a major marketing contract and returning to a myriad of meetings and paperwork at her office. For that memory, she was savoring this small bit of heavenly peace and quite.

As she caught glimpses of the sunset through the tiny holes in the woven straw hat, her thoughts wandered over the past years.

Daniel McInerney, the corporate attorney at Allie's firm, was handsome, witty and charming and they fell in love. After some time, to avoid any potential problems with management, Daniel went on to form his own practice. Two years later they were married and, the following year, their beautiful daughter Caitlin was born. Allie returned to work several months later and her parents watched Caitlin during the day. As time passed and Caitlin was nearing college age, Daniel started complaining of migraines and some days went to the office later or came home early. "Don't you think this has been going on long enough, Daniel? I think you should see a doctor." But Daniel dismissed it as not a serious problem and would see the doctor if it continued much longer or got worse. They had 16 wonderful years together.

Drifting in and out of a soothing sleep, Allie began feeling a breeze. As she removed her hat and looked around, she saw people scurrying to pick up their belongings. The wind was picking up and the clouds were forming ominously foretelling of a storm that was about 15 minutes away. Sun umbrellas were being overturned as beachgoers were trying to close them. *A typical autumn storm. But why on my only day off in three weeks?* She selfishly thought as she tried slipping into her shorts, only to find the wind blowing through them resembling a balloon with short legs. Well, at least she found **that** amusing.

As she chased her hat toppling over the sand, she heard a woman's voice calling, "Excuse me, but I think this is yours." Grabbing her hat, Allie turned to the woman who was approaching her with an outstretched hand holding one of Allie's business cards.

"Oh, thank you," she said to the woman. "It must have fallen out of my pocket. This wind is horrendous."

They both retrieved the rest of their things and Allie started walking toward the parking lot when she heard from behind, "Oh, hello again! It's me again!" as the other woman trotted up to her. "I'm so sorry to bother you, but I noticed your card said you work for a marketing firm here in Calusa."

Allie held on to her hat with one hand as she turned. The woman caught up to her. "Yes, I do. I work for Everything Trending. It's based in Los Angeles but my office is here in Calusa."

"Wow! That's a coincidence! My company is looking to change their marketing strategy and needs some fresh, new ideas. Oh, so sorry. Please pardon me. I was taken off guard with this storm brewing so suddenly. My name is Nora Donnelly." Nora was a pretty, petite lady with sandy blond hair, in her early forties, Allie guessed. Just around her age.

"Pleased to meet you, Nora. I'm Allie McInerney." Allie was attempting to walk forward while the wind was pushing at her back and pulling her beach bag ahead of her. "Listen, would you like to escape this and meet me at Gulf View for a drink? I think being indoors may be a very good idea at the moment." The brim of her hat blew upward exposing her high forehead and tousled brown hair as she held it somewhat secured with her free hand.

"Sure. Yes, I certainly agree with that!" Nora replied. So they both piled their beach gear into their respective cars and drove across the street to the restaurant.

By then, the sky opened up and, with a bolt of lightning hitting the water and an almost immediate sound of thunder, they dashed into the building, drenched but still both intact.

After being seated at a high-top table as far away from the windows as they could get, a Barbie-type blond waitress wearing black shorts and a low-cut white tank top asked them what they would like. Allie responded first. "Give me a vodka martini with a twist, straight up, and make it extra dry please. This storm has my nerves a little rattled."

Nora chuckled. "Make that two!"

The waitress, being 20 or so years younger, found the two middle aged, rain-soaked ladies amusing. Raising her eyebrow, she smiled. "Sure, ladies, coming right up!"

Allie sighed, leaning back in her chair as she pulled her hair back twirling it expertly into a knot.

"So, tell me about yourself, Allie," Nora inquired.

Allie proceeded, telling her she had joined Everything Trending at their Sampa location when she was just out of college. She met her husband there and they were married several years later. They had one daughter who was now 23 and working out of Calusa for a home and business staging agency which required her to work copious hours and travel throughout the US. "With my working so many hours and traveling for my business too, we rarely see each other. So, as a result, we make the most of meeting at times we are both in Calusa as well as other cities in the country when our schedules coincide. That doesn't happen very often, though."

"So, your husband?" Nora asked.

"Oh, yes, my husband. We were so happy; but, then, well into our marriage, I found out he was having an affair and I just couldn't live with it. We divorced soon after."

"I'm so sorry. I shouldn't have asked," Nora replied. "It must have been devastating for you."

"That's okay. But, yes, devastating to both me and to Caitlin. But, someone was watching out for us. Caitlin was able to maintain an amicable relationship with her father. She had always been the apple of his eye. And, after Daniel remarried the 'other woman', she accepted her as best she could. I, on the other hand, immersed myself in my work. That was my saving grace."

"You must be very proud to have such a forgiving daughter."

"Yes. I am *very* proud. She is a unique, fascinating and wonderful young woman and I feel blessed to have her."

Allie glanced down at her hands and then looked up at the other woman. She cleared her throat. "And you Nora?"

She hesitated while the low-top, white-bloused girl placed their napkins and drinks on the table.

"Well," Nora settled back into her chair and took a sip, smiling and raising her brow at the delight of it. "I have lived most of my life in small town just outside of DC. Lived there in the suburbs but had family who worked on Capitol Hill so that brought me into the city quite often. I really enjoyed living in our small community but have to say I loved the excitement and cultural activities in the city. I didn't return to work until after my daughter turned 16. Actually, I have two children. I also have a stepson, Mike."

"Oh, your husband was married before?"

"No," Nora continued, "Mike is a result of his father sowing his wild oats during his senior year in high school," she laughed. "He didn't even know he had a son until Mike was 16 which was quite a surprise to both of us, needless to say. He is a very talented young man in the architectural engineering field. He mainly designs golf courses and resorts. It amazes me he has his father's great sense of style despite the fact he never had the benefit of his influence when he was growing up."

"That must have been difficult for you both when you found out."

"Yes, but we got through it and couldn't have been happier to have him in our lives. He's a great guy and I'm happy to be able to call him my son."

"What does your daughter do?" Allie asked looking over the martini glass to which her lips appeared permanently affixed.

"Kathleen is a partner in a veterinary clinic on a farm in Maryland. They breed sheep dogs and board horses there. Her fiancé, older, is retired from the Air Force. So, when she can sell her half of the partnership, they're planning to move to Florida. I'm really excited about that!"

"It sounds like that would be ideal for all of you!" Allie added. "What brought you to Florida in the first place?"

"My husband and I decided to move to Calusa because Vic had health problems and couldn't tolerate the cold winters of Maryland any longer. And, since I can conduct my business from anywhere, I continued working for the same company, Dress for Success. Very convenient! Calusa is full of fashionable, up-and-coming women who want the advice my company gives. It was perfect for me and Vic was able to continue working for his company in the south as well. But it wasn't long after we moved here that he had to take an early retirement because of his health."

"Have you always worked for Dress for Success?"

"Yes, actually, from Day 1 of my career! I also occasionally volunteer for Look Good/Feel Better for cancer patients so it keeps me very busy."

"It sounds that way. So, the two of you live in Calusa full time now?"

Nora hesitated. "Vic passed away three years ago."

"I'm so sorry, Nora."

"Yes, well, after that I became even more entrenched in my work and it was about a year after he died that I started volunteering for the Children's Homeless Coalition on most of my days off. It certainly does keep me from feeling lonely."

"What a wonderful cause! Where is your step-son living now?" Allie inquired.

"Mike moved to Whispering Heights about the same time Vic and I came to Calusa. His mother had passed and he, like his father, wanted to escape the cold. He actually started his own architectural and building firm there. Whispering Heights seems to be growing by leaps and bounds so he is a very busy young man."

"Do you get much of an opportunity to see either of your children?"

"Kathleen comes whenever she can break away from her work and I usually get up to Maryland a few times a year. It gives me a chance to spend time with her but also gets me into the city to see some of my old friends. As far as Mike is concerned, since he lives only an hour or so away, we spend most holidays together and he drops by whenever he's passing through on business. Both the kids are totally involved with their work so sometimes its hard to connect. But at least there's Face Time and Skype! I'm thankful for that!"

Getting back to their work, Allie said, "You know, I actually remember that several years ago Everything Trending approached Dress for Success hoping we could take over their nationwide advertising campaign. It didn't work out in the end, though, and we lost the deal to a company in Phoenix. It was a big disappointment as getting that account would have been a biggie for us!"

"I didn't know that," Nora responded. "But I do know they may consider you now. Like I said earlier, they are not at all happy with the agency they took on.

"They're looking for a fresher and more modern approach. Would you mind if I had someone get in touch with your firm? Maybe you could put in a good word or two."

"Sure," said Allie, waving the now very soggy card Nora had retrieved from the beach, making an ill attempt to dry it, and handing it back to her. "Why don't you have someone give me a call and I'll see your inquiry gets to the right person."

"That sounds wonderful!" Nora exclaimed. She dug deep into her beach sack but found no business card so wrote her name and phone number on a cocktail napkin, handing it over apologetically.

Allie smiled at the faux business card and said, "I'm sure my firm would love to work with you." At that, Allie looked at her watch and said, "I've got to run, but I'll touch base with you after the connections are made between our companies. Maybe I can get assigned to your campaign. I think it would be fun working together."

Nora nodded in agreement and patted Allie on the arm.

They each threw a 10-dollar-bill on the table and walked out to their cars.

II. Considering the Future

*Sometimes the most ordinary things
could be made extraordinary, simply by doing them
with the right people.*

~ *Nicholas Sparks* ~

Fast forward to two years later. A very close business and personal friendship developed between Nora and Allie. Now 47 and 48, Allie and Nora began talking about their aspirations for the future. They realized the two had always had a similar dream - getting into the hospitality business. Allie had always hoped to open a small B&B while Nora dreamed of a large, rambling inn on substantial acreage. The strongest common ground they shared was they both knew they could work well together and would make a cohesive team. And both were getting burnt out from their high pressure jobs. Each of the women were fairly well set financially, both from their lucrative jobs, as well as Nora having invested wisely in her inheritances and Allie having fared well both with her parents passing and from her divorce from Daniel.

Nora's exciting expectations made Allie's seem lackluster by comparison so she immediately became excited over the big inn concept. She asked Nora, "Where would you find such a large parcel of land to build on?"

"Well, with Mike being in Whispering Heights, I know it's the fastest growing city in Florida. It stretches over one hundred square miles and still has a lot of prime vacant land."

Nora continued, "Most importantly, this fast-growing city so far has no accommodations like what we envision. Given the world-class destination Whispering Heights has become with its Jasmine Hot Springs and pale ontological draw, I think it would be an ideal location. I hear there's a major baseball team looking to relocate their spring training stadium there and hotels and restaurants are popping up everywhere! Since there are no accommodations like what we are thinking, we would be the first. Just think of it, Allie!"

"Actually, Caitlin and I spent quite a few weekends in Whispering Heights at a very small motel at Jasmine Hot Springs when she was attending The Barnum College of Art and Design in Pyakkahachee. I think it would be a perfect spot for an Inn but really hadn't followed how much it's grown in the past few years."

"I know a lot of people who still think of Whispering Heights as being underdeveloped and rural, and it still is in many areas but that only adds to its charm."

"Have you spoken to Mike about this?"

"Yes, as a matter of fact!" Nora replied, beaming from ear to ear. "Mike has been spending a lot of time with Whispering Heights developments along the Coconut Shell Waterway and on Pinnacle and Salt Cove Boulevards. He's told me there is a lot of prime acreage just waiting for the right investors."

Talking about it sounded exciting. But were they willing to move to Whispering Heights from Calusa? What a drastic change that might be. And were they willing to give up their lucrative jobs so soon before normal retirement for a venture that may or may not succeed? They each needed to give it some thought.

One afternoon several weeks later when they were able to meet for lunch, Allie confessed, "Calusa isn't all that big a city but we've both traveled a lot and spent considerable time in some of the largest cities in the country. I'm a little concerned we might be homesick for the lifestyle we're giving up."

"That's crossed my mind as well; but, even though Whispering Heights may be new, it's growing rapidly. I was thinking of a friend of mine, my director when I was in Maryland. She was from a family who owned a Fortune 500 company in the city and lived there most of her life before taking a position as Senior Director at my company. She actually moved from the city and lives and works in a small town outside of Richmond, Virginia called Lightfoot. Who ever heard of Lightfoot?" she giggled. "Anyway, she fell right into the small town atmosphere and admitted it was good for her soul. She found Lightfoot somewhat challenging but easy to recruit new consultants since educated, small-town women were looking for something meaningful to do and earn a good income."

"That's true. Hopefully, we will be able to pay a good wage to people looking for work. I'm a firm believer in treating employees as I would want to be treated, and that includes a decent salary for a job well done!" Allie was beginning to understand how small(er) town living would not only be good for her, but also good for job seekers in the community. Plus, she really needed to get off the corporate roller coaster. It was wearing her down.

"So," Nora continued, "I don't think moving to Whispering Heights would be that difficult and we'd be close enough to quite a few major airports. It isn't that far from Calusa, or Sampa either for that matter. We also have the option of Fort Plyers or Ponce de Leon airports if we have a sudden urge to visit a big city! Oh, and, by the way, I've been reading Ponce de Leon is soon becoming an international airport! Who knows? We may contribute toward making our new home the most trending town in all of Florida!"

"Yes. That's right," Allie replied. "You remember my good friends, the Johnsons. They were at the last few Christmas parties you came to."

"Yes, of course I remember them. Suzanne and Drew," Nora responded.

"Well, they both decided to change careers a few years ago and joined the TSA at Ponce de Leon Airport. Drew has recently been promoted to Chief Security Officer and Suzanne is now in charge of Ground Traffic Control."

"What did they do before they started working for the airport?"

"They both worked in law enforcement," Allie explained. "Drew was a sergeant at the Ponce de Leon Police Department and Suzanne was a free-lance undercover detective. Then, overnight it seemed, they both decided they had had enough.

"There had been two incidents that put them over the top. You may have read about the police officer who shot and killed a young boy at the Seven Eleven when he was reaching in his pocket for his cell phone. The cop had received a call-in that there was an intruder; but, by the time he got there, the guy had already taken off with a handful of lottery tickets. It was argued it was a case of mistaken identity when the officer shot the boy, but he was put on administrative leave while an investigation was being conducted. One week into the leave, the officer committed suicide, leaving a wife and three children."

"Then there was the case of the woman keeping something like 12 or 13 pit bulls at her house. Can you imagine?" Allie continued with disgust as she wrinkled her nose and shook her head. "When Suzanne was investigating some complaints, her sidekick was attacked and mauled by two of the bitches. Suzanne had to put the dogs down on the scene and the owner came running out shouting she was going to 'get her' for killing her dogs. I think her name was Calucci or something like that. A bad news kind of family!"

Nora sat, listening intently. "I had read about those incidences, yes, but never made the connection between them and your friends. No wonder they wanted out."

"You've got that right! Anyway, my point is that I got some inside information from Suzanne recently that United Kingdom Air will be scheduling flights out of Ponce to London by Christmastime and that One Jet will be adding flights to LA, Dallas and Chicago sometime in April. That is going to make Whispering Heights much more accessible to both domestic and international travelers."

"That *is* exciting, Allie! I can envision us advertising at the local airports with colorful, eye-catching framed posters as well as maybe partnering with the airlines to bring domestic and international travelers to Whispering Heights, to our Inn!"

Our Inn, What a nice thought!

Nora was so excited she could hardly contain herself. "Mike just learned he won the bid to design Whispering Moss Golf Course! The design would allow LPGA and PGA qualifying matches and any of the majors to be played on it. He showed them the plans he did in Virginia and they loved it! Of course, they have their own ideas about the specific design but they know he can do it!"

"How wonderful for him, Nora. What a fabulous opportunity!" Allie was so pleased for him and felt the warmth Nora held for her stepson.

"The new course will bring golfers for the winter so we might want to think about offering golf packages to guests."

"That sounds interesting. We'll have to talk to management once they near completion."

"Allie, I think the design of our Inn should coincide with the architecture of the club house, two-story with a veranda on both floors with rocking chairs. Yes! Rocking chairs!

"And how about a secret passageway inside?" Nora continued. "I know that sounds strange but it could be used in our advertising. We could store things for different events and holidays there but think of the fun we would have if we said it was haunted. Maybe we could hide a skeleton somewhere in the room. And we could decorate the grounds in the fall. One time when I was playing golf in Maryland around Halloween, they tied ghosts made out of plastic garbage bags to each flag pole. It helped that it was a foggy morning."

Allie laughed at her friend. "Well, that certainly does sounds fun," she joked. "I do have to say I love the idea of verandas and rocking chairs though."

"Oh! I'm getting off track," Nora giggled. "The most important thing is that the city is subdividing acreage around the course and have put the parcels on the market. Mike told me there is a 5-acre parcel available between Whispering Moss and Great Fossil Pond if we want to look at it. Apparently, someone had attempted to build a home on the property years ago thinking they would build a horse ranch, but the frame collapsed mid-construction. The story goes the owners felt something paranormal was going on and deeded the property to the city. Everyone thought the family was a little strange to have thought that. But, whatever! Do you want to take a ride up and look at it?"

"Wow! That **is** weird." Allie had been listening intently. "But, of course. We should definitely have a look. Do you know who to call for an appointment? I'd like to walk the property and look at the boundaries and what lies to either side. The golf course and Great Fossil Pond would both be great neighbors, but we need to know if there are any other properties in between."

"Good point" Nora added. "I'll make some phone calls in the morning.

As it turned out, the only person they needed was Mike who made the necessary inquiries and received permission to take his step-mother and Allie to the property.

Mike drove up behind them in his pickup, arriving just as they did. He was fully equipped with all he needed. Nora laughed, "Here he comes! I'm sure he has already surveyed the land and has the plat from city hall. That boy is on top of things, to be sure."

Certain enough! Mike got out of his truck with plans tucked under one arm, a clip board in hand and was carrying a small folding table which he set up in front of Nora's car.

At six foot one and of lean build, he carried himself with leopard-like grace. His prominent eyebrows, angular face and dazzling warm brown eyes were a striking reminder to Nora of her late husband.

What an absolute catch for some deserving young woman! Allie thought.

"Hi ladies!" He greeted them giving each a gentle hug. Unrolling the plans and flattening them onto the table, he started explaining the property lines, the location and parameters for sewer and water as well as the city's plans for roads, sidewalks and other utilities.

He explained how the property could tie into the golf course and the overall planned community.

"So, this is where the golf course will be?" Allie was pointing in the southerly direction on the plans.

"Yes."

"Would our guests be allowed to use the course?" Allie asked.

"Yes, again!" Mike smiled. "Even though the course is being built as part of a gated community, access will be allowed to anyone wanting to play golf or to have lunch or dinner at the clubhouse. We might even be able to arrange for VIP guest passes for your visitors allowing them to use the facilities at a discount."

Nora jumped in. "So, we could maybe get passes at a discount from the club and incorporate them into a guest package? And possibly even throw in a lunch or dinner at the clubhouse?"

"Possibly," Mike responded.

Allie nodded vigorously in agreement.

"And look. Right about here," Mike was pointing toward where the clubhouse would be, "we possibly could work with Whispering Moss and the city to build a foot bridge over the canal."

"That sounds fantastic, Mike!" Allie exclaimed. "We would have a ready-made entertainment venue for our guests right at our doorstep. Do you know who owns the land to the east of here?"

Mike explained "That is another 3-acre parcel that is privately owned but it's been uninhabited for years. Apparently, it was willed by the Crocker family to relatives who live in the northwest. It's hard to say why, but for some reason, they aren't interested in selling. Who knows what may pop up over there in the future!" Mike was looking in that direction. "One thing I am certain of is that because the Crocker property abuts Great Fossil Pond, anyone buying that property would have to consult with Pond management because of its sensitive historical paleontological significance."

Nora and Allie were listening intently as Mike proceeded. "As a matter of fact, before you get too far along, it might be wise to set a meeting with Fossil Pond and Archeological Society representatives. We don't want to do anything that might compromise the fragile nature of the site."

"Do you think this will be a problem in moving forward?" Nora asked him.

"I don't know. But I'm fairly sure any expansion they plan will be on the existing property. I understand their future plans are to add a small paleontological museum in this area, something that will serve as an educational tool for students, divers and the general public." Mike pointed to the northwest portion of Great Fossil Pond. "I don't think they will want to buy the Crocker land if and when it ever becomes available. For one thing, I know the funds are not there and, secondly, in talking to the guy who oversees the place, they want it to remain small and contained. There's plenty of room on it to build their museum as well as guided walking trails which is also in their long-term plan. I really don't think your building here will cause a problem but we should still talk to them as future good neighbors. I doubt an Inn, if it ties in with an overall old Florida theme and drainage and lighting are held in check that it will be a problem. I'm only saying it would be the neighborly approach to take."

"Of course, you are absolutely correct," Allie agreed, looking at Nora. Nora nodded in agreement. "So," changing direction (so to speak) for a moment, Allie continued, "It looks like west would be in this direction. Is that the canal?"

"Yes, it leads out to the Pyakka River which will bring you to the Gulf. It's big enough for very small boats and kayaks or paddle boards, but that's about it. Your property will extend west out to the waterway."

"Can you give us an idea of the distances around the Inn as you envision it?" Nora asked him.

"OK. What you have here is practically the equivalent of five football fields! So space is not an issue. Here is your Inn as you proposed it to me." Mike and the ladies were now refocusing on the plans. "Frontage out to the main road is 1000 feet. From the back of the Inn to the canal is about two acres. To the north (toward the golf course), you have another two acres. From the east side of the building, looking to the Crocker property, you have roughly a thousand feet."

"So it looks like we have lots of room for gardens and outside gathering areas. We're thinking in the future we will have various events. If we plan it right, we can keep it natural and enchanting while still being functional. Which leads me to this, Mike. Allie and I are planning to live on site. We envision the space to include a family room, a small kitchen and an office large enough for two desks, computers and a printer along with four bedrooms and three and a half baths," Nora said.

"Yes, and plenty of room for extra shelving and file cabinets in the office," Allie added. "The second two bedrooms would be reserved for Caitlin and other family or friends who come to visit. Would you mind adding all this into the plans? Oh, and, of course, we would need private access as well as the main entrance to the Inn."

Mike was getting used to the enthusiasm of his step-mother and her friend. "Sure. Not a problem. I think your office should be located where you can gain direct access to the Inn. Not only would it be convenient for you but you could meet with your guests there for concierge services, making payments, etcetera. It most likely won't have windows but we can bring in natural light with a few solar tubes."

"I like that! What do you think, Allie?"

Allie nodded heartily in agreement. She was getting so excited she could barely contain herself.

"We were also discussing a small, quaint caretaker's cottage and a shed for equipment and tools. Maybe you could add that somewhere over here." Nora was pointing to the northeast corner of the property."

"We also need to have similar cottages, tiny houses if you will, built for a housekeeper and cook," Allie added. "It makes sense for them to live on site."

"All of that is possible. There's certainly enough space for almost anything you want to do, money being no object," he laughed. "It's good you're thinking ahead. I'll incorporate all of that as part of the overall plan, just so you will get a better idea of space; but we can always whittle it down if we need to."

"Oh, and we do need a secret passageway inside the Inn," Nora added with a wink and a smile.

Allie and Nora were very familiar with the Three Dancing Graces sculpture in Whispering Heights as it was a historical gateway to Jasmine Hot Springs, the one and only tourist attraction at the time the city was incorporated 60 years before. So, the two decided *Inn of Three Graces* would be a lovely, appropriate name and a potential draw, tying in with the history of the area.

III. Peculiar Occurrences

Something was very peculiar as to why the original ranch house collapsed with no apparent reason in its early construction. There had been no wind and obviously fire did not bring it down. There was no evidence of sink hole activity nor was it a question of vandalism.

The area was known for its Indian occupations as was most of southwest Florida, and the whole state, for that matter. Indian burial grounds are abundant in Cavern Creek and artifacts had been discovered at Eagle Point in Eagles Nest as well as Great Fossil Pond and numerous other areas within the county and beyond.

"The owners of Eagle Point Pub are so connected with the Tribal Council that I'm wondering if they know of any other unusual occurrences near burial grounds. Maybe we can take a ride up there for lunch in a few days and see if they have any information to share," Nora said.

"You're right. I understand the pub can't have any repairs made on their thatched roof except by the Seminole Indians so they definitely would have some contacts," Allie responded. "I'll call first to see if either Jay or Todd will be there. I met them both at the Native

American Culture Lecture last month. I hope they will remember me."

The clouds were starting to form in the northern sky as Nora and Allie headed toward Eagles Point. They were both silent, trying to ingest the events of the last few days. They had spent countless hours planning for the Inn's construction and interior design. The structure was to be of old Florida architecture with some interior Native American influences. It had been planned down to the very last details including Seminole patchwork bed coverings and, in the foyer, the original painting *Osceola Holding Informal Court with his Chiefs* by Lucille Blanch. They had purchased the painting from an auction house in Fort Plyers and were delighted to have acquired it for the Inn. All of that was finally becoming reality and the two women were determined to make it happen.

Osceola Holding Informal Court with His Chiefs

~ Lucille Blanch ~

Jay met them as they arrived. He remembered Allie well and greeted them warmly. They explained what they were doing with the Inn and that they were mystified over what happened to the previous owners' ranch collapsing mid-construction for no apparent reason. Jay explained the collapse of buildings around Indian burial grounds was not uncommon in Florida. He spoke of several, the most recent occurring at Buck Point on the St. John's River. He went on to say there has never been any rational explanation for these occurrences.

Todd suggested they contact a gentleman by the name of Don Cypress, a Seminole Tribal Council member who, according to his sources, had a first-hand experience with the collapse of a home he and his family were building.

Construction of the Inn was underway. The land had been excavated and preliminary grading had been done. Nora contacted the Seminole office and invited Don Cypress and a few others to come out to walk the property. In doing so, they discovered a spearhead and said it looked to be from the early 1700s. They agreed to have it further examined and documented and Don would return it via UPS. One of the men suggested Nora and Allie consider inviting Great Fossil Pond officials to the grand opening ceremony and presenting it to them for their new museum.

"What a simply wonderful idea!" Nora exclaimed.

Don was particularly interested in hearing about the collapse of the original house. He explained he and his wife had begun building a home in Ocawa six years before. The excavation brought up numerous artifacts and uncovered several bodies dating back to the early 1800s. After going through a lot of red tape with the city as well as the Tribal Council, they were allowed to begin building. However, almost immediately after the framework was in place, the entire structure collapsed to the ground. He and his family attributed it to The Great Spirit and never pursued the project after that.

This got the two woman a little nervous. Nora spoke to Mike who seemed somewhat amused and suggested they contact their insurance company, *or a psychic*, he thought, just to be sure they would be covered if something 'paranormal' were to happen. It was obvious Mike was much too pragmatic to buy into the unexplained but amused the two friends nonetheless.

As the Inn began to take shape, Nora and Allie were again giving thought to decorating and went to the storage facility where they had started accumulating treasures for the Inn. Since the storage manager had facilitated the deliveries, this was the first time they had been there. It was a local company where they had rented two double pods to house the furniture, paintings, decorative pillows and other items they had purchased.

Clip boards and pens in hand, they set out to take careful inventory. The Lucille Blanch painting was the first thing they saw, barely visible through the bubble wrap it had been packed and delivered in. Historical books about various Native American tribes and the Indian Mounds of Florida were neatly boxed and labeled in a corner of the unit. They had planned to place the books on shelves in the Inn's conversation room for their guests. There were various Seminole sweet grass baskets as well as dolls in authentic Native American dress they planned to position on the back of a chair or on a bed in each guest room. They were beginning to realize they needed to shop for more items.

As they were marking their inventory, Nora called out, "Allie! What *is* this?"

Something was wedged between a slightly opened drawer and the frame of a dresser.

"Oh God! It looks like a dead animal!"

"No! Look! It looks like a wig!"

They drew closer and Allie turned on her cell phone flashlight. She gingerly opened the drawer and, grabbing a fire place iron from its stand, used it to flip the thing over, jumping back and causing Nora to gasp.

"I've never seen one before but, my gosh, it sure does look like someone's scalp. Look here."

Taken aback and somewhat revolted, they called the police.

"Thank you for coming over, Detective Holmes," Nora said after introductions were made. They showed him the scalp and he thought *they called me here for this?*

He remained gracious despite his thoughts. "Very interesting," he said.

Then, taking a closer look, he admitted, "Ladies, at first glance I thought this was a scalp replica that is sold in souvenir shops; but, taking a closer look, it appears to be a real scalp!" Holmes actually surprised himself and took a step back.

"Puzzling as it seems, it looks like an Indian scalp according to the texture of the hair. And possibly a woman because of the length, but not a white man as you might expect."

Allie was nervously fidgeting with her phone and Nora stood white-faced listening to what he was saying.

"Ladies, I have no idea how this may have gotten into your storage space. There is absolutely no sign of break-in," he said while looking around the pod. I'd like to know if anyone else has access to this unit. Otherwise, we need to assume it was in the dresser when you bought it. Do you know the storage owner's name?"

Allie handed him the manager's card.

"In the meantime," he continued "I will take this in to the precinct and have it sent out for DNA. It could possibly lead to an unsolved crime."

Oh my goodness!

Detective Holmes pulled on his gloves and placed the scalp into a plastic bag marked 'Evidence' and neatly recorded the date and place with a few other notes on the outside of it. Both Nora and Allie could see he was in deep concentration and it had nothing to do with what he was writing on the bag.

As he was leaving to go to the manager's office, Holmes said, "There's a man, Dr. Steven Douglas, who is an expert in Native American history. His family is Cherokee but he was transplanted from Oklahoma to Southwest Florida, continuing his education in Native American culture. I'd like to call him in and talk to him about this. Will you both come to the station when I know a date and time?"

"Of course!" they said together.

"No one can get in there," the facility manager emphasized, looking at Detective Holmes. The key codes are changed every time a new tenant signs a lease. Only the current tenant, the facility's owner and the site manager (that would be me) have access to the unit. So, there is no way anyone else could gain access. If they did (or even attempted to), it would be on video as everything is recorded and backed up daily."

"Can I get a copy of your surveillance videos from the time Ms. McInerney and Ms. Donnelly first rented the facility?"

"Of course, but I do need to contact the owner for clearance. I'm sure he will cooperate. I'll personally deliver it to you as soon as I have the recordings downloaded." Holmes handed her his card. "My guess, though, is whatever was put in this pod is what was originally delivered."

He tended to agree on that point.

Holmes extended his appreciation and left.

Allie and Nora stayed to look through the rest of their inventory. They carefully recorded all the items they had purchased at auction and, in a bedside table, discovered an album with pictures and writings dating back to the late 1800s to early 1900s. They took it with them to look at later.

Dr. Douglas arrived at Holmes' office at 2 o'clock the next afternoon. Nora and Allie had already arrived and were sitting, both on the edge of their seats.

Confirming Detective Holmes' thinking, as Douglas examined the scalp through the evidence bag, he said emphatically, "This is not a white man. It is most definitely an Indian scalp. And it is not from the 18th or 19th century as one might expect. This is a relatively fresh scalp. Will you be sending out for DNA?"

"Yes," Holmes replied. The results should take a few days."

"Well, my guess is that this will prove to be the scalp of a Native American woman. And younger as I see no evidence of aging here. Maybe the DNA will determine an approximate age. You do know, I am sure, that there are incidents of scalping where the victims survived. I hope this is the case."

Allie and Nora took this all in. "Did white men actually scalp Indians? I thought it was the other way around," Nora inquired.

Douglas explained that the idea of a settler scalping Indians might seem like a historical quirk. Most Americans assume that if there was any scalping going on in Colonial times, the Indians were doing it, not the English. But Americans most certainly did scalp Indians during and after the Revolution. "They also stripped Indian corpses of their skin," he added.

Whoa! This was something Nora and Allie did not need to know!

Focusing his attention on the detective, Douglas said, "In this case though, if I am correct, this might have been a fairly recent act of violence. Perhaps after your results are in, you may want to check your missing persons list and try to tie in something to determine who this person might be. I would also suggest checking hospitals and doctors' offices to see if someone had sought treatment. I hope you can find her and it isn't too late!"

Detective Holmes was amused by this unsolicited advice. "Of course, that's an *excellent* idea, Dr. Douglas," giving the ladies a wink and a smile.

As Nora, Allie and Dr. Douglas were walking to the parking lot, he thought they might be interested in visiting various Indian sites in the area and suggested if they hadn't visited the Indian Mounds at Eagle Point, it might be interesting to them. "If you are at all familiar with Eagle Point, you know Elizabeth Potter employed people of all walks of life to work on her land. She grew citrus, had cattle and built up her land for her descendants. Look at the small cemetery on the grounds and you will see inscriptions on the tomb stones and the historical society has information on who is buried there and elsewhere. She employed wonderful people of all heritage - African American, and those from South America and the Caribbean Islands as well as Native Americans who helped build the Pyakkahatchee area."

While Dr. Douglas was very knowledgeable, Allie thought him to be quite presumptuous of what they may or may not like to do, especially after just meeting him; but, then again, she knew she could be quite cynical at times. That being said, Nora agreed it would be fun to take a look at Eagle Point. After all, they needed to educate themselves about various points of interest in the area so they could speak with some knowledge to their guests. Perhaps they could pick up some brochures at various areas of interest and leave them on the table in the conversation room as well as in the guest rooms.

So they decided to make a point of visiting the Indian Mounds at Eagle Point as Dr. Douglas had suggested, as soon as they could.

Three days later, Detective Holmes called to ask the ladies to stop by the precinct.

When they arrived, he explained they had identified through DNA that the scalp was of a young woman who had been missing for 18 months when her body was found washed up on the shore in the Balemas. Her name was Kalyani Bowers and she was 16 years old at the time of her disappearance.

"Oh my Lord!" Nora was horrified. "Do you think there's some connection between the origin of the dresser and whoever was responsible for her disappearance?"

"We're working on it. Can you tell me where you bought the dresser?"

"Yes, of course" Allie responded, shaken by what she had heard. "We found it on Big Jim Billie's web site. Wherever he got the dresser, I have no idea."

Trip Crocker was hiding behind the palmettos east of the property, watching Nora and Allie as they met with Mike and the City Inspector. Trip was in his mid-90s and walked with a prominent limp. They had heard he lived somewhere on the old Crocker property and that he and his wife had no children. There were also rumors she passed away suddenly many years before. Trip had been seen around town on an old motorized bicycle picking up dropped fruit to use for food and collecting litter he found along the roadways and sidewalks which he would bury or burn. His parents, like him, were Florida crackers and had worked for Elizabeth Potter. His mother cooked and did other household chores while his father worked in the citrus groves. They were both said to have been buried on the Potter estate.

Detective Holmes, Allie and Nora met with the local auctioneer, Big Jim Billie, at the construction site.

Big Jim Billie, a robust man of about 60 and of Native American descent displayed high cheekbones and almond shaped eyes, large heavy earlobes and an inverted breastbone. He was beaming and anxious to answer questions. Big Jim seemed to know everything about everyone in Whispering Heights and was more than happy to share it!

The dresser's origin traced back to the barn of an old house adjacent to the Inn property and was owned by the Crockers.

He explained that Trip's father was born and raised in the house. After he married, his new wife could not get along with the in-laws. So they moved to the Potter Estate for work and housing. That is where Trip was born and raised. Mrs. Potter apparently had a fondness for the fair-haired boy and took care in home schooling him. By the time he was 12 years old, Mrs. Potter put him to work tending cattle in the fields and paid him handsomely for his efforts.

Big Jim continued, "There was a young Seminole girl who was hired to work the fields. Trip and she fell in love and married when they were both only 15 years old. Since Trip's grandparents were growing old and in ill health and Trip's mother did not like his father spending so much time traveling to and from Whispering Heights, she *suggested*, if you know what I mean," winking at the two women, "that the young couple move into a small chickee on his grandparents' property, right over there."

Big Jim was pointing east. "And, so, the young couple was commissioned to look after the aging grandparents. Very sad that Trip's mother was so selfish.

"The grandparents died within days of each other from the influenza. Trip was the beneficiary of a small monthly annuity and the right to live in the house until he died. The main house and land were willed to a niece. The rest was left to their favorite charity, an orphanage in Pyakkahatchee. Trip's parents received nothing."

"So Trip moved into his grandparents' house after they died?" Nora asked.

"No. While they were all at the funeral, which happened to be a double funeral as it turned out, lightning struck the house and it burnt to the ground."

"How awful! We have never walked the property so wouldn't know if there is a house there or not."

"Why wasn't the dresser destroyed in the fire?"

"Apparently the dresser was being stored in the barn. I don't exactly know how, but it ended up in the hands of a couple who lived in Fort Charlotte and, when they died, I bought most of that estate, including the dresser. About two years go, I sold it at auction."

Holmes was scribbling notes onto a small pad of paper and glanced up at Big Jim over his glasses which were perched on his nose. "Do you know who the high bidder was?"

"Yes, his name was Lucky Calluci. He said he was buying it for his mother's birthday. His father was Tony Calluci. You know, the guy who's been in the news. He's a notorious member of the mob. About a year ago, Tony and his wife were gunned down in the Niami Grand Paradise parking garage. I think it was in March or April. I guess they had been in the Balemas and had some business to finish up in Niami when they returned. Some business, huh? Anyway, I reacquired the piece from one of the Calluci brothers a few months before Ms. McInerney bought it. I have all the documents at the warehouse and can make copies for you."

"Is it unusual for you to not thoroughly inspect the contents of furniture you bring in?" Detective Holmes inquired.

"With the volume we take in, it's pretty hard to check everything," Big Jim responded. "This piece probably wasn't checked because we took in three different estates in the same week besides individual pieces like the dresser."

That seemed logical to Holmes. He was practically dancing in his shoes and his stomach slowly began filling with jitters. Could the late Anthony Calucci have been involved in the Kalyani Bowers abduction, torture and murder? It appeared likely. It sure would tie in with her body being found in the Balemas.

"We found an album in another piece of furniture we bought from you," Allie said, looking at Big Jim. She took it from her tote bag and placed it on the picnic table Mike had brought in, which he had dubbed their "temporary office." They turned the pages carefully seeing a picture of what seemed to be grandparents with a small child on the man's knee.

Big Jim took a closer look at the old photo, pulling a small magnifying glass from his pocket. "If the piece you're referring to was of the same dark cherry Queen Anne design as the dresser, it too would have been originally acquired from the Crockers and eventually auctioned to the Caluccis, circling back to the auction house and then to you ladies."

Nora turned the picture over and, in barely legible smudged ink, they read *Howard*. "I wonder if this is Trip's grandparents with Trip's father when he was a boy," Nora wondered.

"Could be," Big Jim said. "They used to call his father Trip too but I think that was either a middle name or a nickname. So could have been Howard. I don't know."

Big Jim went on to say that young Trip's wife died in childbirth, along with their son. Trip buried her and the child on the perimeter of the two properties. Shortly after, he was thought to have gone mad, his chickee was in disrepair and he lived alone in the barn but was known to have makeshift camps on other parts of the property as well.

So that's why we had heard they had no children, Allie thought. *Trip must have had the child buried but it was somehow not properly documented.*

Detective Holmes, preparing to leave, looked at Big Jim. "I'll wait for those documents from you, sooner rather than later if you don't mind."

No problem. I'll have everything to you by the end of the day."

After the two men left, "Let's call it a day. I need a soak in a hot tub of water and a few glasses of wine."

Nora laughed at her friend. "Watch out or you'll turn into a wrinkled old prune."

"Too late for that!" Allie joked.

"I need a break from everything too. I think I'll call Mike to see if he can do an early dinner and a movie. Something funny. See you tomorrow."

IV. Trip Crocker

It was July and the Inn was nearing completion. Caitlin had been making frequent visits helping to tie loose ends together. Her expertise was invaluable and both Nora and Allie felt fortunate for her input, not to mention her upbeat and spontaneous personality. Mike was especially happy to see Caitlin the times she visited and looked forward to family dinners, mostly at his house where the three women did the cooking, but sometimes dining at Blue Parrot Grill, a newly-opened restaurant in Whispering Heights. Nora and Allie couldn't wait to have the Inn finished and start having Mike and Caitlin over to what they affectionately called "Cook's Kitchen".

Cook had already been hired and was actively planning her kitchen, shopping for china, glassware, cooking utensils and linens. In addition to that, she lovingly brought lunch to the construction crew every afternoon at one o'clock. She first covered the picnic table with a red checkered tablecloth and matching napkins and frequently placed a bouquet of a few fresh flowers in the center. Unpacking her picnic basket, she brought out her famous cranberry, walnut and chicken salad with fresh baked bread and fruit or sometimes sandwiches from the previous night's roast beef, along with her sweet wine vinegar cold slaw. It was always a surprise and the construction workers felt uncharacteristically pampered for that 45 minutes in the middle of their work day. The only stipulation was that they BYOW (bring your own water). They all were quite fond of her and affectionately referred to her as 'Miss Cookie'.

The women had also hired a groundskeeper who was kept busy tidying up after the workers as well as building raised flower beds at the canal side of the property, away from construction, preparing them for planting when the Inn was completed.

Nora had also interviewed several people for the housekeeper position and she and Allie were narrowing it down to the best candidate.

All was going well, *they thought.*

Southern Sun's curiosity was piqued and they wanted to do a story on the Inn. Rumors of the past owners feeling there had been some supernatural occurrence surrounding the sudden collapse of the original building was becoming a talking point in town. So they sent a reporter over to interview Allie and Nora and some of the tradesmen. They wanted to know if anything else had happened that could substantiate paranormal activity on the property.

The ladies were baffled. Nothing had occurred that they were aware of, nor did any of the workers see anything unusual.

But, given the nature of the media and the content of some of their articles, people came forward with stories of strange lights hovering over the area surrounding Great Fossil Pond. Some claimed to have heard strange sounds when they walked by and some said they heard a faint baby's cry, not able to determine the source of the muffled sound.

Southern Sun announced the opening target date was August 15th and it was hoped the Inn would be filled to capacity through the end of April.

Using an artist's rendering of the Inn, Nora designed a full color brochure which they had printed at a local shop. They had provided copies to Bureaus of Tourism throughout Florida as well as Whispering Heights Area Chamber of Commerce. They also hired Everything Trending to market the Inn through Travel & Leisure as well as several major airline magazines.

Southern Sun's prediction came true. The Inn was booked to capacity through the end of April.

The accumulation of furniture in storage had grown, necessitating the rental of another unit. As the movers brought things to the Inn, Caitlin and Nora directed them to where each piece of furniture should be placed. Carefully labeled boxes of bed linens and towels, books, decorative items and kitchen equipment were stacked up in the conversation room awaiting placement. The company they had commissioned for window dressings had staff busily at work and kitchen and laundry appliances were being brought in and installed...a flurry of activity for an entire week.

Nora took a call from Sean Clark who had read about claims of strange occurrences near their Inn. Sean was a docent at the Seminole Ancestry Society and immediately got her attention when he mentioned some paranormal activity at a cemetery on the museum grounds.

As he was on his way to Sandcastle Island on Tuesday, what for him was his Saturday, he asked if he could take a few minutes of their time on his way through.

"Certainly, and I'm sure my business partner would like to hear what you have to say as well."

The ladies were curious and would use the opportunity to ask him about a commemorative marker appropriate for their property.

Sean met them at the Blue Parrot for coffee.

"So glad to meet you both," Sean extended both hands, one to each lady.

"Nice meeting you too, Sean." Nora said and offered him a seat at their table.

Allie nodded and smiled politely.

A very interesting man, Sean had a doctorate in archeologically and had been Curator of Florida's Museum of Natural History in Grainsville and a Professor of Archeology at University of Florida South Central. He and his late wife moved to Johnsonville to be near their children after she'd been diagnosed with terminal cancer five years before. There, she would be able to spend the rest of her life with all the people who mattered most. So Sean decided to go into early retirement and accepted a vacant docent position at Seminole Ancestry Society. Since his wife's passing, he wrote several novels - *Passing Through to the Other Side* and *Memoir of a Native American through the Eyes of an Archeologist"*.

"Allie and I are both very interested to hear what you have to share about apparitions at your museum."

"Yes, after reading about the strange occurrences in Whispering Heights, I thought you would be interested." He took a sip of his coffee and continued. "Strange as it might seem, both museum staff and visitors have come forward claiming to have seen a mysterious figure in various areas of the cemetery. Some said it was a woman and some claim she appeared pregnant. Others have said they have felt a 'presence' of some sort."

"Really?" Nora exclaimed in astonishment.

"Yes, really," Sean replied. "In fact, my son, who knew nothing of previous sightings, was touring the museum grounds recently and claims to have seen her. He said the form was transparent but he could tell it was a woman who appeared pregnant and held her hands over her belly. Other people have come forward with descriptions of similar sightings. The strange thing is that none of this had been publicized up until recently when the press got hold of it through one of the museum visitors. When we get reports of this type, all goes into the confidential archives for future study and nothing is revealed to the public."

Chills ran through Allie's spine. *Could it really be a ghost?*

It was August 15th and the day of the grand opening was upon them. All last minute details had been attended to and there were fresh flowers in every room. Freshly-baked cinnamon and raisin scones were ready to be put out and tea kettles were whistling in the kitchen.

Caitlin had used her staging expertise to help furnish the Inn with timely accessories that could be changed out as the trends and seasons warranted. She added flameless candles with timers in all rooms as well as indoor Ficus trees with small fairy lights in the common areas, all adding an ethereal atmosphere throughout the Inn.

A myriad of citizens turned out: Chamber of Commerce officials, photographers and reporters from the Southern Sun and Herald, as well as the City and County Commissioners. a local state representative and four Seminole Tribal officials, including Don Cypress. A contingency representing Great Fossil Pond and the Southern Florida Archeology Society were also present for the sphere presentation. Even Detective Holmes, Sean and Big Jim showed up.

The first guests of the Inn were scheduled to arrive the following day but several came in early for the ceremony and were staying at a nearby hotel. It was a perfect day, 82 degrees with puffy white clouds against a bright blue backdrop. Everything seemed perfect and Nora and Allie couldn't be happier.

At dusk, the two sat in rockers on the veranda sipping minted ice tea and recounting the events of the day as well as anticipating their first guests the following afternoon. The marketing they had done was successful and the Inn was booked to capacity. Cook, the housekeeper and groundskeeper were all living on site and loving their jobs. Both Nora and Allie shared in administrative duties, overseeing the property, staff and marketing.

There was still a faint light in the sky. Nora noticed a figure hovering around the palmetto patch. "DID YOU SEE HER?" he shouted. It was Trip Crocker. Both were startled by this and stood up in unison, walking to the veranda's railing.

"Mr. Crocker, is that you?" Nora asked. "Won't you please come over and join us for some iced tea and cookies?"

They called to him again. Finally a figure emerged from behind the palmettos. He walked with a prominent limp, his small frame hunched, and he carried an old, battered hat.

"Hello missus," he said.

"Mr. Crocker, is there something wrong? What can we do for you?"

"Don't like nobody on this here property."

"We have nothing but respect for this property and we would like it if you were pleased to see we have done so much with it," Nora responded.

"Too close."

"Too close to what, Mr. Crocker?" Allie asked. But he retreated behind the bushes, not answering her question.

They wondered if that was the end of it, took in a deep breath and settled back into their chairs.

A short time later, Nora said, "Allie, I was approached by a Chamber member this morning and the City is thinking of naming a park and the new library Three Graces to further instill its significance in Whispering Heights."

"That's a wonderful idea! It looks like we have started something. It's such a lovely sculpture and the name sounds so calming and inviting. Three Graces could be a big part of the City image, more like a mascot in a way. I can envision a facsimile of Three Graces on every major entrance to Whispering Heights."

"Oh, and wouldn't that be a wonderful name for a day spa or salon?"

"Or a nature trail along the canal!"

Allie went on without waiting for a continuation of the bantering of thoughts. "You know, there's something Mr. Crocker said when he saw us. Do you remember he said 'did you see her?' Do you remember hearing him say that?"

"Now that you mention it, I did hear that. What do you suppose he meant? Do you think he saw a vision of his wife? You do remember what Sean said about sightings of a woman walking the grounds of the

Ancestry Society? And what we learned about Trip burying his wife and baby along the line of the two properties?" Nora was speaking so rapidly her heart was pounding. "Both times we have seen him, he's been hovering around the palmettos over there." She turned her head and nodded in that direction. "Do you suppose that's where she's buried and he goes there to be near her?"

"Who knows, but that could be what he meant about our being too close - which reminds me, we were so involved with everything else that we never looked for the graves Big Jim told us about. What do you think about getting up before dawn and taking a look?"

The ladies walked silently to the palmettos at six o'clock the next morning. They hoped Trip Crocker was a late riser; but, lo and behold, they saw Trip, his back to them and his hands outstretched in a contemplative mode. The ladies quietly scurried back to the Inn. They didn't want to know what might happen if he saw them.

"I think we should call Sean Clark. Maybe he'd be willing to pay Mr. Crocker a visit and draw him out."

At nine o'clock that morning Allie called Sean who was amenable to talking to the old man but didn't hold out much hope given his peculiarity. Rather, he offered to do a talk at the Inn about Indian fact and lore the following Tuesday. Maybe Trip would come out...just maybe.

They set a time with Sean. Nora went to the Southern Sun and called the Southwest Herald to see if they could get some coverage the day of the event. Allie called Channel 6 TV and was promised a reporter and camera crew would be there.

They wanted to keep it small so only invited a few to the gathering, including guests who were staying at the Inn and asked the press to respect that, to which they graciously complied.

It was to be held under the live oak canopy at the east end of the property and the ladies made arrangements for small round tables and chairs for up to 35 people. Tablecloths had been ordered from Rental Supply and the local florist had been notified, all to be in subtle Indian motif. Cook was instructed to begin testing Native-American dessert recipes. They planned to have a buffet table where guests could help themselves to lemonade and sweets.

The groundskeeper was happily intent on trimming and weeding the morning of the event until he came running up to the house, banging on the door. "Miz Nora, Miz Allie!" Josh was clearly out of breath and shaken.

The two offered him a seat and a glass of water. "What is it, Josh?" Allie asked.

"I wuz chippen da grass o'r dare." He pointed to the oak hammock. "End I seen a laddy holdin a bahby. Den she dispeered in da busses! I prayed ta da Good Laud I wazin gone crazy."

REALLY? But how appropriate to have this happen just before the event!, The ladies thought.

Sean was right on time. As it turned out, somehow the word got out and 83 people from the area showed up and no one seemed to care they didn't have a place to sit. Fortunately, there was plenty of standing room and Cook had made an extra few gallons of lemonade and plenty of sweets which she had planned to freeze if there was anything left.

Some people had their own stories. One lady spoke about three people having been murdered in a freezer at the Cracker Barrel in Calusa and her son's apparition while working the night shift there.

Another from Venicia and a man from Lacadia both also shared stories, one of cold breezes and taps on the back, and the other of a vision of his mother who appeared much younger than when she crossed.

A couple from Colonial Willisburg was vacationing and said they and their daughter had attended the nighttime ghost tour there, seeing firsthand that the Peyton Wandolph house was truly haunted.

Sean launched into his talk. After fifteen minutes, from the corner of his eye, he saw a small stooped man carrying a battered hat and thought that was probably who the ladies told him about.

"Sir, would you like to come and join us?" The man took one small step forward.

"Mr. Crocker? Do you have a story to share?"

The man shyly began telling how his wife and baby died in childbirth. They had been gone for many years but he still visited their graves every day so that he could be near them.

"I dug graves 'or yonder." He pointed toward the palmettos to the side of him. "I go see them all the time. Sometimes they visit me too."

What? Nora and Allie thought.

The audience was mesmerized and listened thoughtfully, full of empathy for the sad-looking old man.

"Can we do something for you?" Sean asked.

Trip just bowed his head and shrugged his shoulders. *Nothing will bring my family back*, he thought.

The cameraman stepped forward and Trip retreated behind the palmettos.

Just then, a man from the audience spoke up. "I'd like to suggest someone contact the city to see if they will donate a monument for the graves. If not, I would be willing to contribute the funds to do this. I heartily believe this will validate his family and perhaps bring him some peace."

Trip heard this from behind the bushes and bowed his head, bringing his hat to his heart.

> *Some things, I wish I didn't see.*
> *Like space between, you and me.*
> *Recall how close we used to be.*
>
> ~ *Valormore De Plume* ~

Later, speaking to Nora and Allie privately, Sean said, "I would like to pay Mr. Crocker a visit after all the guests have left and ask him to join us for tea, if that's ok with both of you."

Sean was a man in his early fifties, not movie star material, but nice looking and obviously took care of his health. Mesmerizing hazel eyes with a bit of graying at the temple but still with a full head of hair, it made him noticeable in a crowd. Since losing his wife five years before, he had gotten on with his life, completely immersing himself in his work while also appreciating how precious life can be.

He continued, "I feel that one of you should join me. He knows who you are and it may make a difference."

"If you think it would help, I would be willing to go with you," Allie said.

Nora broke what seemed to be a silent few seconds. "That's a good idea. I'll get the staff to clean up and see that our guests are comfortable. We will have tea ready in the conversation room for a possible meeting with Trip. Following that, we plan to prepare small sandwiches and coffee to serve our guests around four o'clock. Hopefully your schedule will allow you to join us, Sean."

Nora, Allie and Sean met with Trip in the conversation room. Trip was noticeably uncomfortable and, with so few teeth, it was difficult to understand him. What he explained was that this was sacred Native

American land and he didn't like the Inn's guests roaming the property. He thought it disrespectful and uncomfortable.

"Where do you live Trip?" Sean asked.

From what they deduced, the chickee had deteriorated and fallen and he was unable to rebuild it because of his fragile state. He slept on the land which had belonged to his grandparents, in a barn on the property or camping wherever he could find shelter. He was homeless but wanted it that way. There was nothing anyone could do to help him other than to perhaps offer him food, clothing and blankets. They guessed he bathed in the stream and bought what little food he needed with his meager inheritance. When they suggested social services might be of assistance, he just shook his sad head.

Just then, at Nora's prior request, Cook brought in a brown bag containing a roast beef sandwich, a large container of juice and some small, warm poppy seed cakes and handed it to Trip. "We hope you will take this small gift from us, Mr. Crocker." He accepted, nodding his humble head in appreciation and left.

"It's so unfortunate so see such a lost soul," Sean commented. "Hopefully, he won't make his presence uncomfortable for your guests."

"I don't think so," Nora replied. "I feel we may have befriended him in some small way."

Diagram of a Chickee Hut

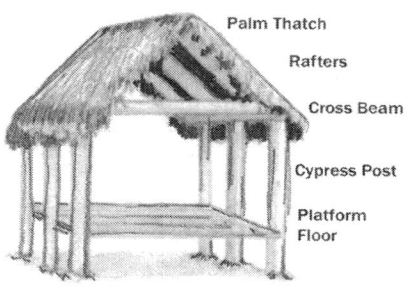

Lights were out in the common areas at 10 PM with the exception of a few flameless candles and the dimly lit Ficus trees. The outside lamp post was glowing and the weather was perfect for a little stroll in the softly lit garden; but then the sound of crashing glass came from the dining room. A brick had been thrown through the side bay window.

Allie called the police who were there in five minutes. The commotion thankfully didn't disturb any guests since no one from the guestrooms appeared.

It was Detective Holmes who rang the doorbell. Officer Trabor accompanied him. "Please come in, Detective, Officer." Nora was waiting in the conversation room and they then escorted the officers to the window that had been broken.

After discussing the events of the day, Officer Trabor asked directions to where Trip lived. Allie said she had gone out to his camp sight with Sean Clark and explained approximately in what direction they should go.

"We will have to wait until daylight to look for him. But I think we can walk a little way into the woods now to see if there is a campfire or a lantern glowing that will tell us if someone is out there. "We will be taking the brick to the station with us."

The officer and detective tipped their hats to the ladies and said they would be in touch. "But, for tonight, board up that window and be sure your locks are secure."

The groundkeeper had been awakened by the police lights and said he would get some boards from the shed and secure the window for the night.

The window was replaced by noon the following day. By mid-morning, the story of the smashed window at Inn of Three Graces was a hot topic in town.

Detective Holmes and Officer Trabor paid a visit to Trip the following morning. They questioned him, wanting to know where he was the previous evening at 10 o'clock.

"Don't have much sense for time at night," he apologized. "Just in daylight. I follow the sun but don't know much about the moon."

He continued, "I seen Ms. Allie and Ms. Nora and Mr. Sean 'round mid-day, then went to see my wife and baby. Ms. Nora was nice to give me food so I come back here," he pointed to his poorly structured camp, "to eat and to sleep." They totally believed him.

"Is somethin wrong? Are they awright?"

"Yes, they are fine, Mr. Crocker. Did you hear or see anything last night?"

"There's always comins and goins 'or yonder with the Inn 'n all. I seen car lights comin up the road to the house kinda late and then heard the car leave a spell after but seen no car lights then."

Holmes was aware of several vandalisms near archeological sites throughout various towns in Florida. He looked up the Seminole Tribal Council whose headquarters were in Halleywood. The web site listed names of those in charge and he was able to get through to the Vice Chair who confirmed some renegade tribal members were vandalizing property on or near Indian burial sites throughout parts of Florida and the Council was investigating through their own sources to stop it. This was a long shot but Holmes thought it might be possible this may have been the case with the Inn's window being broken as well as several recent vandalisms near Jasmine Hot Springs.

For now things seem to be calm and the next four months passed without incident.

V. *Fun Daze*

Allie placed an ad in The Southern Sun for their first Ladies Fun Daze and were inundated with phone calls and e-mails. Their web site was now operational and they were getting a lot of bookings from that as well. The first event was to be held February 8th. The guests were to arrive with caftans and sans bra and were prepared to laugh and have a good time. Their instruction sheet said to bring some fun anecdotes of their lives and to be prepared to sing songs and dance the hula. And just maybe they'd have a firsthand encounter with the Inn's ghost.

Cook was busy in the kitchen and Josh was manning the roast pig that had been wrapped in banana leaves and secured with chicken wire. A large hole had been dug in the ground and the logs had turned to hot coals. All that needed to be done was to pop an apple into the hog's mouth to allow heat to get through (the ladies had no clue until they asked) and lower the animal onto the coals. It amazed the women how much Josh knew about this ancient method of pig roasting. He explained that traditionally the pig was then covered with dirt but he thought better of it and covered the pit with a large sheet of metal. He anticipated it would take 18 hours to roast. "Dis gone be crazy goowd, mizzes!" he grinned.

The grounds of the Inn were decorated in Hawaiian motif, complete with tiki torches and brightly-colored paper lanterns, grass skirt tablecloths and raffia placemats.

Centerpieces of fresh flowers flowing out of bright Hawaiian mask vases and fresh plumeria leis placed at each seating added to the ambience.

A tiki bar was positioned at center point with brightly colored red, blue, yellow and green high-top tables and chairs positioned around it, all of which had been obtained from a local rental supply company.

The five guest rooms were prepared as nine of the 48 ladies attending had purchased the extended package, including overnight accommodations with breakfast the following morning. Four of them agreed to double up even though they didn't know their roommates, only wanting an opportunity to stay at the Inn.

The first guests began arriving at 4 pm. They were very excited to be away from home and their ordinary routine if only for a short while. Those who were staying at the Inn were escorted to their rooms while the others were shown to a changing room. Out they came in their colorful caftans, their jewelry as exciting as the outfits. One lady had multiple elasticized jewel bracelets covering her upper arm with long, dangling copper earrings and a brightly-colored muumuu. Another was wearing a peacock blue, green and yellow caftan and matching hat with peacock feathers. All were dazzling displays of artistry and color. By 4:30, all were assembled and ready to have a good time. The temporary hired waiters passed pineapple, strawberry and cheese skewers and an array of brightly colored drinks complete with paper umbrellas.

Mike volunteered to bartend for the evening. Needless to say, he got a lot of attention from the 60- and 70-something ladies...not to mention a few taps on the butt.

What a good sport my stepson is, Nora thought.

And Allie just giggled over every encounter he experienced.

One lady who spoke up was from Buffalo and regaled everyone with her tales of how crazy she was about clothes. She always brought an extra suitcase when she traveled so she could take home all she bought. Nora definitely could relate to that lady!

Another was amusing them with her husband-mistress stories. They were caught kissing at a polo game and she divorced him 'practically on the spot!' *Kissing,* Allie thought. *What about finding them in bed together?* But she just took it all in, sat back with her coconut rum punch and enjoyed the fun of it all.

Yet another woman who was visiting from abroad had been on tour in Florida discovering haunted inns and had come to Whispering Heights after hearing of the Three Graces' ghost. She went on to explain she and her late husband had purchased a 200 year old house in Marduff and, from the moment they moved in, there were bizarre things going on. Apparently, a woman had been slain in an upper bedroom more than a hundred years before but her spirit never left. They witnessed peculiar phenomena like nailed-to-the-wall closet hooks being turned up-side-down and strange noises coming from the bedroom where the body had been found.

She told of one of their cats having been buried in her back yard. When work was necessary on the septic area, it disturbed the cat's grave. Later, on several occasions, when she opened the back door to the garden, she had to step back, realizing her cat, translucent in form, was scurrying past her and scampering up the stairs to the front bedroom which is what he had always done when alive.

Very chatty indeed, she went on to explain that she has had 'visits' from her late husband on occasion, always at the breakfast table on Sunday mornings.

Funny, she looks perfectly normal to me, Nora mused.

Nora and Allie both felt as though they were attending a party, not one they were hosting. It was so much fun for both of them!

When darkness fell, the tiki torches were lit and dinner was served. There was a wonderful buzz of conversation and laughter under the oak canopy. Many were feeling mellow from the cocktails but had made arrangements with the Inn for van transportation back to their homes or hotel. Those who were staying at the Inn had no worries either. Everyone was in a happy, festive mood.

One of the local guests, Sue Long, suggested they consider building a playhouse at the Inn. She had been a playwright in New York before retiring to Florida and offered to write two-act mystery comedies for them. Another, a retired fashion designer by the name of Eleanor Parker, said she would design and sew costumes.

Another piped up saying she would help with publicity and tickets.

Since they all knew about the ghostly hauntings, it was proposed a resident ghost be worked into the advertising. Both Sue and Eleanor were willing to donate their time and services if Nora and Allie were willing to offer a small percentage of the profits to a local homeless charity.

No problem there! Nora and Allie were very charitably minded.

They promised to give this some serious consideration. Both felt the idea was exciting and also quite feasible since both Sue and Eleanor were local. The main thing they would need to do, besides getting all the necessary permits, would be to have a stage and seating built and lighting and sound installed.

Thankfully, there was Mike!

Later there were tears as one woman said she so badly needed this outing. When her son committed suicide two years ago, she fell into a deep state of depression. This event was better than any psychiatrist or grieving seminar she had been to...and she had been to many.

So happy this has been a positive experience for you! Was Nora and Allie's combined thought and gave a sad smile to the woman.

That night, there was a shadow creeping along the hallway. Two of the guests saw the apparition. Were they just imaging it? No. Both saw it at different times when they got up in the night and compared their sightings at breakfast. Both saw the same thing...a man with a woman holding a child. This was an exciting addition to the breakfast conversation!

It was 10:15 the following morning and Detective Holmes, accompanied by Officer Trabor were escorted to the kitchen where Nora and Allie were discussing new recipes with Cook.

"I'm afraid we have some sad news for you," Holmes said. "Two boys were hiking the land next to you and came across a camp sight that appeared abandoned. As they continued their trek, they noticed vultures flying low in the sky. Upon investigation, they discovered a body. It was Trip Crocker."

"Oh my God!" Allie exclaimed.

Later, the two, saddened by the news, sat rocking on the veranda recounting the events of the party and what fun it had been for them. And now this!

After a moment of silence, Allie said, "I was thinking about what our two guests had seen last night in the hallway. Do you suppose it was Trip and his family? Maybe he feels comfortable here now that he's joined his wife and child."

"Yes, that makes sense. I think I'm beginning to believe in all of this and would like to think he's still with us. Maybe after the police clear this as a natural death, we can arrange for burial next to his family."

We'll have to call Sean. He'll know what to do."

Trip was buried next to his family with little fanfare. Allie, Nora, Caitlin, Mike and Sean were the only people attending. Sean had arranged for Trip's dates to be inscribed on the monument and they all stood quietly as the grave was filled with earth.

As they prepared to leave, three feathers blowing in the breeze landed on the graves. Sean picked them up, handing them to Allie. "These are sacred feathers of eagles and are important in the eyes of Native Americans because they believe the eagle can fly closest to the creator."

Trip Crocker and his family were together, though Trip had a little unfinished business, as they would later learn.

The ladies who had attended the first Fun Daze spread the word and the phone was always ringing. A month later, they held a second event. The group that came was in the mood to see a ghost and in a silly frame of mind. Four of them put together a Platinum Girls of Whispering Heights skit, complete with wigs and fashion depicting Brianna, Rene, Sondra and Dotty. It was hilarious and set the stage for yet another successful evening event. These women certainly did have some imagination!

From then on, Fun Daze was held monthly bringing in guests from Sampa to Calusa through Southern Group Tours. Southern Group marketed the day trips, complete with bus transportation, and incorporated the Ghost of Trip Crocker into their advertising. Others from the area merely booked the event through the Inn and some arranged overnight getaways so they could have the potential advantage of a ghostly nighttime experience.

One morning at breakfast one of the guests said she believed she saw a ghost in her mirror. Nora and Allie both wondered, *Did she really see something or was she wanting it so badly that it seemed real?*

It was now nearing mid-April and the heat of the season was already becoming intense. Workers were contracted to install misters in the gardens and under the oak hammock to keep guests comfortable for the upcoming Fun Daze season finale in May.

The season was proving to be very busy, with every room booked every day of the week through the end of June.

VI. *Farm to Table*

Nora and Allie were having lunch in the kitchen with Cook when the idea of hosting a farm-to-table dinner event came up. Allie mentioned an article she had read about a local organic gardener and personal chef, Alice Garland.

That afternoon, Allie contacted Alice and made an appointment for her to come to the Inn the following day. They talked about using farm-fresh fruits and vegetables but also starting a vegetable garden and fruit grove on their property. Alice voiced that they may consider hiring a gardener specifically for that purpose. "But, if you hire someone to do this," she joked, "will he find any bones or arrows when he's preparing the soil?"

They smiled at her and went on to talk more about hosting the farm to table dinner monthly on a day when the Inn was not typically full during the summer. They agreed that Wednesdays would work best and Alice was excited and agreeable to helping them, suggesting they may want to feature some foods grown on Three Graces property.

After Alice's visit, Nora placed an ad for a fruit and vegetable gardener.

Jerome was originally from Ohio and from a long-line of farmers. When the family farm suffered hardships and his family passed, he, his wife and two sons moved to Florida to start a cattle ranch. At the ranch, the three men prepared the soil for planting vegetables and a citrus grove, all of which they lovingly attended along with their cattle.

Their sons were grown and married now with boys of their own, all able bodied and knew the business inside and out. Jerome and his wife, Suchi (the Indian name meaning being able to carry on), now in their mid 50s, were looking for a quiet place to live which was near their family. They were hired and a small house was constructed at the back of the property, as well as a shed and greenhouse, alongside Josh's already existing tiny house and tool shed.

The house was perfect for Jerome and Suchi. Suchi worked her gardening magic and planted flowering shrubs around their house and seasonal flowers in window boxes to make the home more attractive. They loved the idea of living on the grounds of the Inn and enjoyed their new job. Yes, it was their home now.

The high school contacted Nora and Allie. It was suggested they consider horticulture and culinary students alternate working in the greenhouse and gardens to gain more knowledge and extra credit.

Alice also encouraged the students to plant mango, avocado and citrus trees in common areas such as at city hall center, the library and city parks. She explained that the trees would provide food for those who were hungry, avoiding spoilage and accumulation of rodents, all while they would earn school credits and learn to give back to the community.

She also suggested Allie and Nora consider donating a percentage of their farm-to-table profits to purchase trees for the students' project which they readily agreed to. The ladies also suggested to the school they choose two different culinary students each month during summer break to work with Cook in planning and preparing the farm-to-table menus.

Alice, Nora, Allie and Cook had put a program together and the ladies began advertising with Southern Group Tours, on their web site, social media and with the local newspapers.

Invitations were printed and mailed to their clientele and to various members of the community, printed on Inn stationery. This was so exciting!

Inn of Three Graces   *Lazzeri & Doyle*

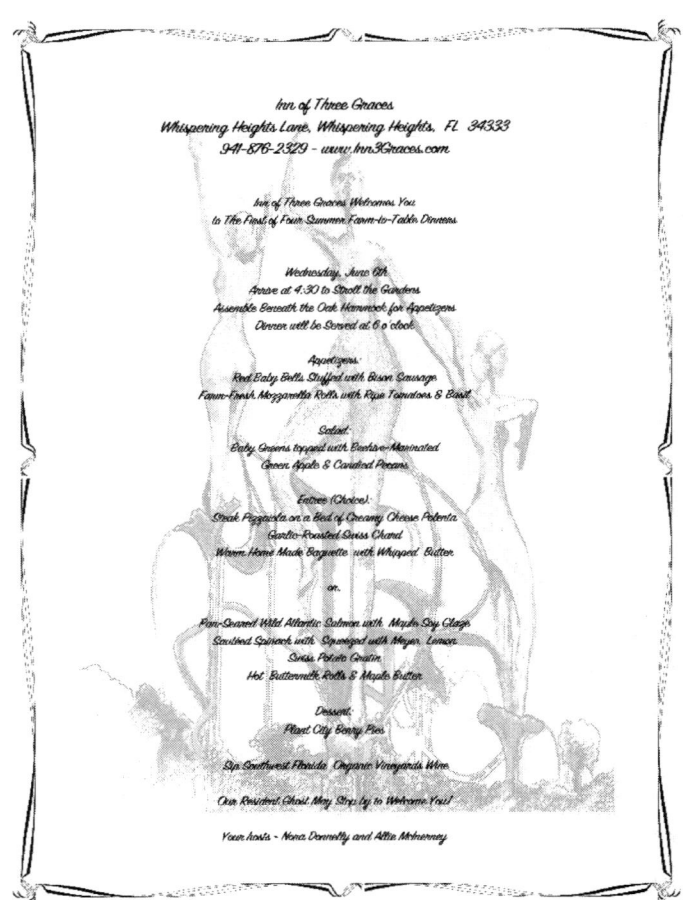

Inn of Three Graces
Whispering Heights Lane, Whispering Heights, FL 34333
941-876-2329 - www.Inn3Graces.com

Inn of Three Graces Welcomes You
to The First of Four Summer Farm-to-Table Dinners

Wednesday, June 6th
Arrive at 4:30 to Stroll the Gardens
Assemble Beneath the Oak Hammock for Appetizers
Dinner will be Served at 6 o'clock

Appetizers:
Red Baby Bells Stuffed with Bison Sausage
Farm-Fresh Mozzarella Rolls with Ripe Tomatoes & Basil

Salad:
Baby Greens topped with Beetive-Marinated
Green Apple & Candied Pecans

Entree (Choice):
Steak Pizzaiola on a Bed of Creamy Cheese Polenta
Garlic-Roasted Swiss Chard
Warm Home Made Baguette with Whipped Butter

or

Pan-Seared Wild Atlantic Salmon with Maple Soy Glaze
Sautéed Spinach with Squeezed with Meyer Lemon
Swiss Potato Gratin
Hot Buttermilk Rolls & Maple Butter

Dessert:
Plant City Berry Pies

Sip Southwest Florida Organic Vineyards Wine

Our Resident Ghost May Stop by to Welcome You!

Your hosts - Nona Donnelly and Allie McInerney

The announcement went on to say that guest rooms at the Inn were limited but arrangements had been made at the Whispering Heights Embassy Suites for anyone wanting to stay overnight. They also negotiated a reasonable rate with The Embassy, including shuttle service to and from the Inn and breakfast the following morning at the Suites. Obviously, the first reservations requested were for a room at the Inn. In total, 102 people responded.

Inn of Three Graces   *Lazzeri & Doyle*

VII. Daniel

It was approaching August 15th, the Inn's first anniversary. In recognition of the event, Nora and Allie commissioned a local sculptor to create a (smaller) version of The Three Graces at Jasmine Hot Springs, complete with a lighted fountain. A plaque was to be mounted to the base of the fountain inscribed *"Three Graces: Faith, Love & Hope - Whispering Heights, FL 2018."* It was installed under the pergola in the northwest garden, acting as a beautiful and restful area for guests. Several benches had been strategically placed for relaxation and meditation. They were very pleased that this turned out so well - another major draw to their property and further recognition of Whispering Heights' history.

"This is unbelievable!" Allie said. "We have not missed a beat since the snowbirds left."

"You know what I'm thinking," Nora predicted.

"Of course I do. You're thinking we should call Mike about adding the three additional guest suites we've been talking about."

"Don't you think we should add five?"

Both were giddy but a little overwhelmed at the thought. They would need to hire additional help for Cook as well as another housekeeper and perhaps someone to help Josh with the grounds and overall upkeep of the property. Additional furnishings and decor along with bedding and linens would need to be purchased, all requiring additional space at the storage facility.

"We are getting calls from groups that want meetings at the Inn," said Nora. She flipped her notes. "So far, a couple of writers' groups and an annuity company have called; and, oh, Innkeepers of Southwest Florida and Hospitality Havens have also inquired."

"Yes, and I forgot to tell you," Allie added. "Cook took a call from Southwest Florida Cosmetic Surgeons when we were out yesterday afternoon. They are looking for a venue for some of their Pyakkahatchee County marketing presentations. Apparently, they hold these events monthly for about eight to ten prospective clients."

"Maybe we could exchange our meeting room for a

free facelift!" Nora joked.

Allie laughed. "It seems like a small meeting room would work for us. I'm thinking it might be a good place to hold guest orientations as well."

"I never thought about guest orientations but it sounds like a good idea! It seems we've been really informal about that sort of thing. We will need to talk to Mike about adding this to our plan, maybe big enough to accommodate about 12 people?" Nora added.

"I think that would be about right," Allie replied.

"By the way, a woman from a local second hand shop called. She has some things we might want to add to our decor. She said she has some Native American pottery, prints and a few artifacts she just acquired."

"Is that the shop on the corner of Alamanda and Miami Trail?"

"Yes, it's called Second Time Around."

Picking up their purses and a set of keys, off they went.

Jodi had a very warm, welcoming personality. Her shop was masterfully arranged with memorabilia of the Seminoles, Choctaw, Calusa and Miccosukee Tribes. When questioned about the Seminoles, she explained that the Seminoles were not originally a single tribe. They were an alliance of Northern Florida and Southern Georgia natives that banded together with people from the Creek, Miccosukee, Hitchiti and Oconee tribes in the 1700's to fight European invaders.

She went on to explain that later the alliance became even closer, and today the Seminoles are a united sovereign nation, even though their people speak two languages and have different cultural backgrounds.

"That's very interesting. I didn't know that," Allie said.

As they were walking around the shop, they noticed a life-size statue of an Indian. "That is a very impressive work of art," Allie observed. "Where did you get it?"

"I found it at Big Jim Billy's on-line auction site. It's apparently a piece depicting a Seminole warrior and dates back to the late 18th century. It was the strangest thing that happened, though." She took a breath, looking perplexed. "One morning when I came into the store, the Indian was turned 90 degrees from where it had been placed. Very strange since no one but I have a key to the store, and nothing else had been moved." Jodi used an upward hands gesture with a puzzled look on her face.

"In what direction was it facing?" Nora asked.

"Actually, let me think," Jodi was mentally

determining north and south from the place the Indian was standing. "Northeast. It was definitely facing northeast."

"So that would be in the direction of our Inn?" Allie asked.

"Yes, it would have been facing northeast toward your property."

It seemed the three had bonded an immediate friendship. It was one o'clock and none of them had eaten lunch. After the ladies had purchased framed prints for each of the five new guestrooms, along with postcards they planned to place on each of the rooms' bedside tables, Jodi flipped the sign *back in one hour*, locked up and followed Nora and Allie to the Crêpe Masters for lunch.

They had noted Jodi's very striking Native American features - high cheekbones, lustrous long black hair and a tall, lean physic.

She went on to talk about her ancestry. Apparently, her great-grandfather married a Seminole girl in the early 1900s. They had two children, a boy and a girl. The boy (Jodi's grandfather) became a cattleman and citrus grower, becoming quite wealthy for the time. The girl married but died in childbirth. "She, I guess, would have been a distant aunt of mine." Jodi said.

"Do you know what her name was?" Nora asked.

"Yes," Jodi replied. "Her name was Hachi Cromwell. She married a Crocker. He's the one I recently saw in the obituaries."

"Yes, Trip Crocker lived on the property adjacent to ours."

Sue came bustling in that afternoon full of plans for the playhouse. "Since the entertainment venues in Southwest Florida are testy about approaching their performers for the Inn playhouse, and I don't blame them, I'd like to suggest we form our own Whispering Heights Thespians Group. I've found a retired New York actor who would be willing to teach acting. What do you think ladies?" She was so excited her sentences were running together. Then, after a deep breath, she waited for an answer.

"Hum," Nora thought for a moment. "To be sure, that sounds like a good alternative to approaching performers who work at other playhouses. Maybe we can also advertise for local amateur performers to come and audition."

"Yes, and what about the possibility of contacting the local college to see if any have a theatrical internship program?" Allie added.

"All great ideas! Why don't you run with it, Sue! Maybe there's a drama teacher at the high school who might also have some ideas."

Nora was thumbing through a program for upcoming plays in Venicia as she added, "Or maybe we could get some of their drama students involved. They wouldn't necessarily have to act. Just being behind the scenes might be good experience for them."

Jodi called from the second hand shop. "I just found a Ouija Board in a box of items I bought at an estate sale. Want to come over and see if we can contact Trip?" she jokingly asked.

Well, this certainly did intrigue the ladies. "That sounds like fun!" They were there in 15 minutes!

Jodi had cleared a low table and placed three pillows on the floor for seating. The Ouija Board was positioned on top of the table and the three just stood there, staring at it for a long moment. Maybe they were going somewhere they didn't really want to be.

"Well ladies, who wants to give it a try?" Jodi, settling herself onto one of the pillows, was anxious to see what would happen.

"Jodi you go first as you are in a way related to Trip," said Nora. They positioned themselves on the pillows and leaned forward as Jodi placed her fingertips on the planchette and waited to see what would happen.

"I didn't know the man, but I'll give it a try."

Jodi took a breath. "What do you want to say?" The pointer didn't move and Jodi gave a perplexed look, raising her eyebrow. But slowly it began moving toward the W, then I, then F, then E. Was this Trip's wife trying to contact them? *What in the world?* their looks said to each other.

"Whose wife? Does she have a name? What is it you want to tell us?" Jodi asked and peered steadily at the planchette as it began to quiver. It began moving again, first slowly to the A, and then slid rapidly across the board and stopped. "Is there more you want to tell me?"

"*NO,*" said Ouija.

Jodi looked up and shrugged her shoulders.

"Jodi, do you know if Trip has any other ancestors? Surely there must be more out there. Are they in this area do you think? This WIFE could be any wife. What if it is someone who is still living and it is a warning of some type? What if this WIFE is in danger?"

She laughed at that. "Seriously?" But then thought *This was **my** idea, after all. I shouldn't tease!* "I'm not really sure about Trip having any ancestors other than his parents and grandparents. But I do seem to remember something about his grandparents having a niece they were quite fond of."

Nora had taken the morning to go clothes shopping, something she said always cleared her head. Allie was in the kitchen with Cook and Alice, going over the menu for their next Farm-to-Table event, when they were interrupted by the housekeeper. There was someone at the door asking to see Allie.

As Allie approached the front entrance, she stood dead in her tracks. "Maria! What are you doing here?" she heard herself ask.

"I was wondering if I could speak to you."

Saying nothing, she gestured toward the conversation room. Allie closed the door behind them and offered her a chair. Maria took a seat and Allie continued standing. "What do you want?"

"Daniel died."

"WHAT?"

"He had a massive stroke on Monday and passed away on Wednesday at 1 in the morning." Maria's voice was unimpassioned.

"Did you call Caitlin?"

"No. She's **your** daughter," she answered indignantly. "I thought you would do that."

Allie detected a faint smell of whiskey on her ex-husband's wife's breath. She was momentarily speechless.

Maria continued, "I need to ask you something."

Now what's coming, Allie thought.

"Well, actually, I want to tell you something first. I was sitting beside Daniel's bed at 12:30 the morning he died. He had been unconscious since the stroke. All of a sudden, he opened his eyes and said, 'Tell Allie I'm sorry'. Then he closed his eyes for the last time. He never got over you and I really have to say I resented you for that."

Allie thought ***YOU** resented **ME**? **YOU'RE** the one who broke up my marriage! This woman is clearly deranged!*

Ignoring Allie's mortification, she continued, "I was just a convenience after you threw him out. He needed someone to be on his arm at parties and corporate functions and I was handy, so he married me. Plain and simple!"

Without comment and clearly dazed, Allie said, "You want to ask me something?"

"Yes." At this point, Maria became noticeably uncomfortable. "Daniel had read about the Inn and actually had done extensive research on the goings on. Every article in the Southern Sun was meticulously cut out and put into a scrapbook. You know, the events, the expansion, the ghosts. He was obsessed by it." She cleared her throat and continued.

"Daniel always wanted to be cremated, but I'm sure you know that. He had told me in a note, in his own handwriting, that he wanted his ashes scattered at Inn of Three Graces. That's what his request was and I can show you the note if you don't believe me." Maria reached for her purse.

"That's not necessary," although Allie had no reason to believe anything this woman told her.

The room was silent for what seemed like a long few seconds. Then Allie said, "As you may know, my business partner and I own this Inn together and I would not make that kind of a decision without speaking to her first."

Maria stood up. "Sure, of course." She scribbled a phone number on a piece of paper and left it on the side table. "You can reach me at this number. Oh, and here's the name of the funeral parlor. That's where he is," she said, handing a business card to Allie. She stumbled a little in her stilettos as she walked out not saying another word.

Allie closed the door behind Maria and leaned against it. "Damn!" she murmured. As if she didn't have enough going on! She didn't need her dead ex-husband roaming the property too!

She looked at her watch. It was 4:30. Caitlin was on assignment in Phoenix so she would still be working. Allie decided to call her that evening after she had returned to her hotel. It would not be easy breaking the news.

Caitlin, now 26 and still single, worked for a very successful Interior Design company based in Calusa, servicing individual homeowners but mostly hotels and resorts across the country. She had worked her way up the ladder and was now VP of Nationwide Operations.

Allie picked up her cell phone and called Nora. "Hi, where are you?"

"I'm just leaving Macy's. I got a call from the Country Club. They have some things for the homeless coalition so I'll be stopping there before coming home."

"Why don't we meet there for an early dinner?" Allie did not want to have the staff overhearing any of this until (and if) they were ready to tell them.

"Great idea! You know what hard work shopping can be. I'm famished!"

On her way to the Club, Allie recounted the events of the past.

Because of the predicted closing of the Orange Skyline Bridge due to high winds and heavy rains that afternoon, Allie was forced to leave work before travel became a problem. Calling for Daniel as she entered the house, she expected he would be in their bedroom napping. He had called her early in the afternoon that his migraine was worse than ever and was going home. She quietly opened the bedroom door but what she saw was definitely not what she expected - Two people, scampering around the bedroom trying to find their clothes, she realized her husband was having an affair.

Stunned, she only said, "Daniel, please meet me downstairs; and, YOU, get out of my house!" It was Maria - 8 years before.

Allie took the house and half of their investments, he kept his retirement fund and the dog. Caitlin was in college. And Allie was alone.

Caitlin flew into Ponce de Leon, rented a car and drove to Whispering Heights. She was incredibly upset about her father's passing, as well as remorseful she hadn't spent very much time with him in recent years.

The ashes were delivered and the ceremony was held under the pergola with The Reverend Miller offering a few words and a prayer. Allie held Caitlin's arm as they walked together, Caitlin scattering the ashes over the gardens. Maria did not come.

The following week, Caitlin received a phone call from her father's attorney in Ponce de Leon. He invited her to hear the reading of the will. Allie went along to keep her company.

They were shown into the attorney's office and invited to have a seat. The smell of old books which lined his bookshelves permeated the air. No one else was present. The folder on his desk was labeled "Daniel McInerney". He proceeded to take out the will and read, "I, Daniel McInerney"....and finished with "leave all my personal effects, including my home, and all bank and investment funds to my daughter, Caitlin McInerney." An addendum to the will listed all personal property as well as bank accounts, stocks, mutual funds and other investments. Caitlin looked puzzled.

"Why wouldn't my father leave his assets to his wife?" Caitlin asked. Allie wondered the same thing.

"Oh, I thought you knew," the attorney said. "Daniel and Maria were divorced. All that was settled in the proceedings." He hesitated for a moment, cleared his throat, stood and said he would leave them for a few minutes of privacy, closing the door quietly behind him.

"That's so strange," Allie said. "When Maria came to tell me about your father's death, she didn't say anything about being divorced from him, yet she said she was by his side when he died!"

Caitlin was staring at the open folder on the attorney's desk, not responding to her mother. Suddenly she found herself seated in his chair looking through the papers in the file until she found a document entitled 'Divorce Decree'. Daniel divorced Maria for having an extramarital affair. Behind that were several copies of e-mails between the lawyer and Daniel. Daniel was asking advice as to whom he might contact to do some investigative work. That must have been how he finally determined she was cheating on him.

The two could hear the attorney talking to his secretary from outside the room. Caitlin quickly put the papers back in order and returned to her seat. Just then the door opened and he walked around his desk to take a seat. He explained the process for distribution of assets, gave Caitlin his card and said he would be in touch with her within a few days.

On their way home, Allie wondered, "Why do you think Maria was with your Dad when he died? Do you suppose she felt guilty? Or maybe wanted to see if she could get him to sign something over to her?"

"I have no idea, Mom. From what you've told me, she isn't a woman to be trusted, but maybe it would be best not to over think this whole thing."

The plans for the Inn's expansion were finalized. The ground was broken on January 17th and the Chamber, Southern Sun Newspaper and local TV station, along with several city and county officials and guests staying at the Inn were there.

"What was that?" The cameraman appeared startled. Everyone looked in the direction he was pointing. Only Caitlin saw what the cameraman saw - an opaque image of a man walking toward her with outstretched hands, and then disappearing as quickly as he had appeared. Her father.

The cameraman did not have his lens pointing in that direction.

Mike was anticipating completion by November 15th when the majority of seasonal visitors would be arriving, many of them wanting to stay at the Inn and to take advantage of the healing waters at Jasmine Hot Springs.

They were totally booked through the end of May, unlike the year before when things started slacking off by April 30th. They had made the right choice in expanding. The Embassy Suites on Salt Cove Boulevard was filled to capacity and turning people away.

Shops were popping up everywhere, restaurants were being built along the winding canal, all having outdoor patio seating and some offering evening entertainment; and a quaint downtown area was nearing completion. Most importantly, all was within walking distance to the Inn. All was good in Whispering Heights and all was good with Nora and Allie. They were excited, busy and happy.

During the construction, they did what they could to keep their guests comfortable and unaffected by the noise of the construction. They turned on soft music throughout the common areas and served breakfast in the sun porch to the far side of the expansion work rather than in the dining room. There, guests had a perfect view of the gardens on the southeast side of the property. The ladies had arranged for all work to stop at 4 o'clock so that tea could be served under the pergola. Not only were the guests unaffected, but they were very interested to see and learn about what was happening at the Inn.

The women had been interviewing for extra help, all of whom would live off site. They had it narrowed down to two candidates for each position, an assistant cook, a house maid and someone to help Josh with the grounds.

Fun Daze and Farm-to-Table events continued, all while the addition was being worked on. Jerome and Suchi had harvested the remaining seasonal vegetables; and, while Suchi canned the bounty, Jerome prepared their gardens for fall planting.

Caitlin decided to take a leave from her job and spend it with her mother and Nora, getting ready for the expansion's grand opening. And she was loving working with Mike. She and Nora were of the same mold when it came to shopping and design. So, together, they took a ride to Niami, stopping in small towns along the way in search of perfect items for the new addition.

Whenever they spotted a potential buy, they would video call Allie so she could see. Yes, she loved it - or no, maybe not. They all respected each other's opinion.

Often Allie would come up with a brainstorm and text them. All in all, it was working.

Supervising the addition as well as attending to the guests and working with the help on her own had become overwhelming for Allie. Nora and Caitlin had been gone for two weeks and had just left Niami, expecting not to return for another few weeks.

"Hi, Nora. If you don't mind, I think I'm going to bring some of the new staff on a little early."

Nora knew what Allie must be dealing with and felt guilty. "I think that's a wonderful idea, Allie! We like all of the candidates, so why don't you decide who you want to come on board. We will be home on Tuesday."

Allie was relieved to hear this but said, "No, take your time. I can manage if I get our help on board next week."

In the meantime, Allie had refused several dinner invitations from Sean. Over that, she was feeling a bit sorry for herself but thought *all for the greater good.*

She was thankful, though, that Nora and Caitlin had taken on the task of finding unique and interesting items for the new guestrooms. This is something she would not have enjoyed doing nearly as much as they did.

Suchi was a wonder with decorating for the seasons and had placed bales of hay with pumpkins, gourds and scarecrows around the main house in addition to assembling a glorious wreath for the main entrance.

Smaller wreaths were placed on the doors of the greenhouse, the shed and the small houses.

Josh, expressing his appreciation, noted "Date loowk crazy fine, Mz. Soochi. I'z mitey glad you does it!"

The days were getting shorter and the heat not as oppressive so Caitlin spent quite a bit of her free time in the garden area sitting under the pergola. She would read in silence, looking up whenever she felt a gentle breeze or saw a butterfly pass by. Waiting. Waiting for her father to pay her another visit.

Let's get a Ouija Board!" Caitlin announced that afternoon.

Neither Nora nor Allie had mentioned the Ouija session at Jodi's so were very surprised by Caitlin's suggestion.

That evening Caitlin, Nora and Allie sat around the Ouija Board. Caitlin had lit candles which were placed strategically around the area.

They all giggled a bit at the oddity of it all. Caitlin placed her fingertips on the planchette. It didn't move, but suddenly, an aroma permeated the room. It was Daniel's aftershave. The distinctive scent of Canoe hit Caitlin's senses first. She was stunned. Allie looked in astonishment as she experienced the same scent.

Nora took her turn. She asked, "Daniel, we feel you are with us. Do you have something to tell us?" The planchette moved to W I F E. *What?* Nora looked at Allie. "Is there something else?" The planchette moved slowly to the A. This was the same thing that happened at Jodi's shortly after Daniel died. Could it have been Daniel, not Trip, as they had thought?

"Why don't you try, Mom?" Caitlin asked.

The cursor was still positioned on the A. "Daniel, who is the wife you are talking about?" She kept her fingers lightly on the pointer, barely touching it, when it slowly moved to Y O U. Shivers ran down her spine and the candles flickered and went out.

After a moment, Caitlin said, "I feel he wants your forgiveness. Are you ready to do that, Mom?"

"Yes," said Allie, and she proceeded to tell him so.

Early the next morning, Allie and Caitlin were having coffee under the pergola. They were both absorbing the beauty of the garden when they turned toward the sunrise. There they saw a tall misted male figure facing them and pausing before turning toward the light of the sun and walking into it. Daniel had received the forgiveness he needed and was now able to cross over.

*You will forever be with us and
show us your undying love
Unforgotten angel from above
Angel with graceful wings
has taught us as a family
many things*

~ Miranda James ~

VIII. The Playhouse

The Inn expansion was slightly ahead of schedule and the construction was now slated to be completed just after Halloween. The Playhouse was finished - a "miniature amphitheater", Mike liked to call it, and they had begun promoting the schedule of performances for the season.

Sue and a writer-friend of hers had written several 2-act plays, all comical mysteries. The first would open in February and would run six consecutive Saturdays. The second would start the beginning of April. Hopefully before then, they would determine if this was to be an ongoing event throughout the summer and beyond in which case new material would need to be written. They also considered doing reruns of in-season performances during the summer months.

It was determined some of the costumes and accessories as well as stage settings could be reused for different plays which would cut down costs considerably. Sue and Eleanor had contacted the retired actor Sue had referred to, and he agreed to volunteer teaching and mentoring performers as well as filling some of the cast positions when needed. All three had interviewed drama students at the local high school who would be working for credit, as well as intern students at Southwestern College of Drama. Some retired people who had a love for the arts also came forward. All were aspiring actors willing to volunteer their time. Those they chose were auditioned and, if they had potential, there was no time wasted in working with them. In the meantime, Eleanor continued to design and make all the costumes. A friend of theirs who was a retired contractor offered to donate his time to build the stage sets.

My, Sue and Eleanor certainly had the connections it took to make this work! Nora thought.

The Inn of Three Graces Playhouse was ready! And it was opening night.

Three parking attendants were in position, tree lights were twinkling and the local paparazzi were waiting to capture the actors and guests as they arrived for Opening Night.

The first to arrive was Dame Deanne who was to play a cross dresser. Dame was wearing a sequin-covered champagne gown and a faux fur stole, shoulder sweeper earrings and a blonde Marilyn Monroe wig. Slinking up the walkway, he gave the reporters something to write about as his sultry voice called out, "Honey, you ain't seen nothin yet."

Bailey Andrews and Shellie Babson were to play the part of a middle-aged woman and a young co-conspirator.

They, too, were already in costume. Eleanor Parker had done magic with her artistry and sewing! Shellie, the younger of the two, arrived wearing retro style white high-waist sailor shorts with a white sleeveless button up blouse, a navy and yellow polka dot hair scarf; and, on her feet, white and blue sheer ankle socks and yellow Lula open toe heels. Bailey, playing the part of the middle-aged woman, looked chic and savvy, wearing a retro white and red floral cap sleeve shift dress, bright red lipstick, a wide-brimmed white hat, sunglasses and red and cream patent leather pumps.

The first scene opened on the deck of a ship. Dame, meeting Bailey and Shelly, looked them up and down, accessing the excellent choice he had made for his first caper. "Well ladies, are you ready for our little escapade? The man you are going to fleece is right over there at the bar." He pointed in that direction with a gracefully extended, jeweled arm. There were giggles from the audience. "You ladies certainly look innocent enough. I'm absolutely certain he will never suspect a thing."

With all the hype about the Three Graces ghost, Sue and her writer friend decided they would engage an actor to play the part of Trip Crocker's ghost and incorporate a ghostly image into the play.

Bailey sauntered across the room and wiggled herself onto the bar stool next to the distinguished looking gentleman, her targeted victim of the evening. She directed her attention to the bartender. "I'll have an extra dry martini, shaken not stirred with a twist." Taking her first sip, she glanced over the glass and batted her eyelashes at Trey Jollay, the retired actor from New York, who was playing the part of a wealthy widower.

Bailey knew her role was to play up to Trey and then steal his valuables; but just as she started cozying up to him, a ghostly-looking figure bumped into the waiter causing him to drop a tray of drinks on them.

"Close the curtain, close the curtain!" Sue shouted from her Director's Chair. *What the hell! This wasn't supposed to happen!* she was thinking.

The actors heard the audience laughing. "Let's just go with it. The audience loves it! Let's say the ghost did it." The actors concurred.

"So sorry, Madam, Sir," the waiter apologized. Handing the two a stack of napkins, he went on, trying to pick ice cubes out of Suzanne's cleavage. The audience roared. "I can't remember anything like this happening before," the waiter babbled. "I am so sorry. It was as though someone tipped the tray and the drinks fell off," all this being said as he dabbed a napkin on Suzanne's lap.

One of the men in the audience shouted, "There's a drink dripping down her legs!" At that, the waiter got down on all fours, licking Suzanne's ankles and working his way up, periodically looking at the audience with a grin. When he finally got to her knee, he lifted her skirt to assess the damage, turned to the crowd and lifted an eyebrow, taking on an elfin look of innocence. The audience was about to start rolling in the aisles.

Sue just threw up her hands. This was not the play she had written, but the actors were doing an excellent job ad-libbing...*and it was funny*, she admitted to herself. Hopefully, they would get back on track with the plot. Suzanne and Bailey were thrown for a loop. As actresses, they knew how to extemporize but this threw the plot of the play to rob Trey into chaos. The script called for distracting Trey so that is what they intended to do in the next scene.

Leaning into him seductively, Bailey attempted to dab some of the liquid refreshment from where it had spattered on Trey's face and shirt.

The spotlight went to center stage as a cabaret singer appeared in a strapless black dress and fuchsia-colored flower behind her ear, long gloves and faux diamonds on her ears and arms. Bailey and Trey were seen in a darkened corner of the room chatting intimately.

The singer began a short medley of numbers starting with '*Til the End of Time*. She received a standing ovation but everyone was anxiously watching Bailey and Trey as the curtain closed at the end of Scene I.

Nora, Allie and Sue were wondering as much as the audience what would happen next.

Guests mingled between scenes, sipping champagne and nibbling on tiny white truffle sandwiches, chatting and laughing about how wonderful the evening was going. Others talked about what wonderful things were being done at the Inn and yet others enjoyed jesting about the Ghost of Trip Crocker.

Scene II went off with out a hitch. Trey's wallet was missing and, as he discovered it, yelled, "I've been robbed! My wallet is missing!"

Shellie ran up to him, appearing she wanted to help. "You're the man I saw at the bar. There's a phone over there. I'll call security."

Ship Security arrived, questioned Trey and then Shellie.

The lights then returned to the bar area where other passengers were eagerly waiting to see what was happening after hearing the commotion.

"I saw that lady with her arm around you," said one of the ship's guests as he pointed to Bailey who was standing nearby.

A ghostly figure of an old man wearing a battered hat suddenly appeared and pushed Shellie into Bailey's path. At that, Trey's wallet fell from Bailey's purse. It was the Inn's *real* ghost. Trip had returned in full thunder. It seemed he wanted to partake in the fun and help the Playhouse succeed.

Bailey was escorted away by Ship's Security and Shellie wandered off.

The cabaret singer began singing *Some Enchanted Evening* when the sound was slowly turned down and the lights dimmed on her. The focus was once again on Dame and Shellie conspiring with yet another female passenger who was wearing a one-shoulder Grecian dress and a spray of faux diamonds pinned to the top knot of her dark hair. Maybe they could finally pull off a robbery!

~*The End*~

The mock Ghost of Trip Crocker, dressed in an opaque veil, had consumed too much rum and was asleep on the lawn behind the playhouse. He would be relieved of his duties in the morning and a replacement would be found....as a backup in the event Trip wanted to take a night off.

The next day the Southern Sun Theater Critic who had been in the audience boasted of the ghostly play and *planned* chaos at Inn of Three Graces Playhouse and the fabulous time everyone had. No one knew it was not the way it was supposed to be. At the end of the review, he said, "Be sure not to miss the next scheduled play the first Saturday in April, *Weekend at Three Graces* - another comical mystery that will leave you rolling in the isles.

IX. *More on the Crockers*

Nora, Allie and Alice were having coffee at the kitchen table when Caitlin charged in all out of breath.

"Mom, Nora! You will never guess what! The parcel next door is up for sale!"

"The Crocker property?" Allie asked.

"Yes! I called the realtor and she said Trip's grandparents had willed the property to a niece. They apparently made arrangements for Trip to live on the property until he died. The niece also passed on and left the property to a daughter in Oregon who doesn't want it so put it on the market. Can you imagine? We have all that beautiful land right next door! I want to buy it and make it a part of the Inn estate!"

"That's very enthusiastic of you, Caitlin," Nora said. "But whatever would you do with it? And remember you have a job you have to return to. How long did you say your leave of absence was?"

"They're expecting me to return in another month but am thinking of handing in my resignation. I'd like to work here with you," she hesitated, "if that's okay with you, of course."

"Of course it's all right with us," Nora assured. "Allie?"

Allie was stunned. How wonderful that her daughter wanted to participate in the business. It's something she had never imagined.

"That would make me so happy, Caitlin; but are you sure you want to give up such a fabulous job?"

Sean Clark saw the play review and called to congratulate them. He needed an excuse to talk to Allie since he couldn't understand why she had refused two dinner invitations from him. He also had an added excuse to call as the Ancestry Society had received a packet of letters and documents referencing the Crocker family and it's ties to the Potters. They were found in a house that was for sale in the Johnsonville area and he offered to share their contents. Nora and Allie didn't hesitate to make an appointment to meet with him at his house the following day, his day off from work. Naturally, both Allie and Nora were curious and they invited Caitlin to tag along. What information might they learn from these letters?

It was a Tuesday morning around 9:30 when they ventured out, using the GPS as they got closer to his address. Sean lived in a lovely Key West style beach cottage on Casey Key. He greeted them wearing shorts and a t-shirt and no shoes. *My*, Allie thought, *he looks so handsome.*

He showed them to the back porch overlooking the Gulf where he had placed a box containing file folders on a table. All three thought the view magnificent but immediately turned their attention to the box.

"Have you looked at these?" Allie asked. "Yes," he responded. "There are some things you might be interested in seeing. I'd rather you look than having me tell you."

Nora and Allie gently began taking documents and mementos out of the box. Caitlin sat beside them quietly, listening and watching. There was a picture of a young Indian girl Nora was holding in her hand. On the back of the picture, it said Hachi Cromwell Crocker - 1937. "That was the year we concluded Trip married," Allie said. "I wonder if she was pregnant at the time the picture was taken."

They then came across a birth certificate bearing the name Edward Cromwell Crocker III, born April 23, 1938, son of Trip Crocker and Hachi Cromwell Crocker. Location of birth: Home. Searching further, there was a death certificate, reading Hachi Cromwell Crocker and Edward Cromwell Crocker. Date of deaths: April 23, 1938. "That certainly does verify the information Trip had given us, that his wife and child died together in childbirth," Sean said.

"Yes, but why were they buried with no documentation on public record?" Allie wondered.

"I don't have an answer to that, Allie; but sometimes in those days, things tended to fall through the cracks. For example, I don't think I've ever heard of two deaths being recorded on one certificate. That might have been why it got lost in city records."

"I wonder who this is," Nora said. It was a picture of a young boy with blond hair and beautiful big blue eyes wearing a battered hat. When they turned the photo over, they saw 'My Wonderful Little Trip' written in a lovely cursive script.

Looking further, they found a letter with the same beautiful writing. It read:

The sixth of October, nineteen hundred forty-nine

To my cherished staff,

I am deeply saddened to inform you of the passing of Howard (Trip) Crocker. He will be laid to rest along side his loving wife, Mabel, in the Potter 'family' cemetery.

The Reverend Danny Schultz will officiate at the burial site on the eighth of October and we warmly welcome you to join a celebration of life at 8 o'clock that morning.

Most fondly yours,

Elizabeth Potter

So it seemed, Elizabeth Potter had a fondness for little Trip Crocker and saw to it her loyal employees, Trip's mother and father, were laid to rest at Eagle Point.

Sean couldn't get over the similarity between Allie and Caitlin. *Truly mother and daughter*, he thought. Both the same beautiful shining brown hair, chestnut-colored eyes and high cheekbones, and both with lovely lithe frames.

Distracted by Sean's gaze on her, Allie spoke up. "Let's stop at Eagle Point on our way home. I'd like to visit the cemetery."

The grounds were very well kept, but extremely old. They carefully read the inscriptions on each grave. Finally, they came across the places where Trip's parents had been buried. The stones read:

> Mabel Elizabeth Crocker, wife of
> Howard T. Crocker - 1903-1938

> Howard T. Crocker, husband of
> Mabel Elizabeth Crocker - 1901-1949

On their way back to Inn, Nora gently tapped Caitlin's shoulder from the back seat. "Have you worked out your plan for the Cottages of Three Graces yet?" She was referring to Caitlin's idea of building small cottages on the Crocker property they had purchased.

She turned to Nora whom she had affectionately dubbed her Aunt Nora and said the cottages were foremost in her mind. "Yes, actually, I've started to work on some sketches that I'd like to pass by you and Mom."

She was thinking tiny one-bedroom cottages, each with a small sitting room, bookshelf and fireplace. Interior design would be of pastel colors and Laura Ashley fabrics. French doors from each cottage would lead to flagstone patios with paths connecting to existing walkways and gardens around the adjoining property. She also expressed her vision of gingerbread trim, flower boxes hung beneath the windows and hanging baskets on each light post at the end of the walkways.

"That sounds fabulous!" Nora exclaimed. "I don't know how busy Mike is with his business but my guess is things slack off for him in the summer. Would you like me to ask if he would help with the planning and building of the cottages?"

"Oh, yes!" Caitlin responded. "That would make it even more fun! Thanks, Aunt Nora." Caitlin liked the thought of working with Mike.

X. *Maria*

It wasn't long after they arrived home when a white BMW convertible with the license plate *Daddy's Girl* on it, sped up the driveway to the Inn door. Out of the car came a woman in a flowery silk dress and a floppy red hat, sun glasses and spike heels. Nora opened the door to greet her. "Are you the owner of this Inn?" she asked.

"I am co-owner with my business partner, Allie McAllister. My name is Nora Donnelly."

"Oh, yes," the woman replied, "good 'ol Allie!"

"Excuse me, but what did you say your name is?" Nora asked. She couldn't get over this woman's rude behavior.

"My name is Maria Calucci," the floppy-hatted woman answered. She smelled heavily of whiskey.

Hearing the commotion, Allie came out onto the veranda. "Maria! What are you doing here?"

Slurring her words, "Now, now, *Allie*! What kind of a greeting is that? But, since you asked, I am here to get what rightfully belongs to me."

"What are you talking about!" Allie was clearly agitated. And why was her name Calucci and not McInerney? *Maybe she remarried?*

"You have a piece of furniture that belongs to me."

"What?"

"The dresser you got from Big Jim Billie."

"We bought several pieces of furniture from Mr. Billie's auction house. I'm not sure what you're talking about."

"You know what I mean! It's the hand-carved cherry dresser. It's mine and I want it back!"

The dresser the scalp was in, both Nora and Allie thought.

"I'm sorry, Maria, but I purchased that item at auction. And if it was yours and you wanted it, why did you put it up for auction? It belongs to the Inn now."

"I didn't want to sell it!" She answered belligerently. "It belonged to my mother-in-law and she promised I could have it when she died. So now she's dead and my husband's sleazy brother sold everything when we were in the Balemas with my in-laws. He did it so he could make a few bucks and skip on us!" Maria was wobbling in her too-high-heeled shoes.

"So that sounds like something you should take up with your brother-in-law. I'm afraid I can't help you," Allie said. Quivering inside, she had all she could do to maintain her composure.

"You just wait and see, bitch! You will be sorry you ever built this place!" And, with that, Maria got back into her car and left, leaving rubber tread marks on the drive.

So that confirms what Big Jim Billy said about Maria's in-laws being in the Balemas around the time the dresser was sold, Allie thought.

Nora was baffled by the whole incident. Allie was now visibly shaking.

They agreed to call Detective Holmes. Maria certainly couldn't be so stupid as to demand the dresser if she was aware of the scalp. Could Maria's in-laws really have had something to do with the missing girl? Did her mother-in-law really promise her the dresser?

It certainly seemed that way.

"Allie, let's go see the Calucci B&B."

"Are you insane, Nora? I think she's a crazy woman. And, besides, what would we accomplish?"

"Maybe she won't be there; and, besides, I'm curious."

"But what if she **is** there? What will we say? What is our excuse for being there?" asked cautious Allie.

Nora, being the rouge of the two, responded "Really, Allie! What can she do...shoot us or something? Just say we were rethinking the dresser and want to talk to her to see if she was willing to negotiate a price."

"But I don't want to sell the dresser. I love that dresser."

Please, Allie. Lighten up a little. We aren't going to sell it to her. Our price will be too high."

Nora winked at her friend and the two got into the Inn's van. Nora jokingly prayed, "Trip, **please** come with us." She looked at Allie and laughed. Just then a breeze inside the van ruffled their hair.

"Trip is here," Allie said, smiling. "Now I feel better about going with you."

Paradise B&B was three streets from the end of the Harbor Bridge and had lovely curbside appeal. There were a few cars in the lot but most guests, like at their own Inn, probably left for the day to explore the area. The two-story teal blue building had a roof lantern cupola and widow's walk overlooking the harbor. The Internet description of Paradise B&B said that it was built by a ship's captain in the early 1900s. The story told that he was a pirate who stashed his loot somewhere in the house and kept women and plenty of rum to entertain himself and his crew.

They knocked on the door and a woman who they did not recognize answered. They stepped inside and asked for Maria but she was not at home. They glimpsed beyond the foyer to see a darkened room with ornate furniture and heavy brocade drapes. A middle-aged man with graying hair was sitting in a wingback chair by the fireplace with a drained brandy glass by his side, his fingers nervously tapping on the upholstered armrest.

"We are on assignment writing a story about the pirate who used to own this house," Nora blurted out. "We wonder if we might take a look around inside."

Allie kicked her gently on the ankle.

"I'm afraid that won't be possible," the woman responded. "Leave me your card and I will ask one of the owners to contact you."

"Oh, that won't be necessary," Allie responded while grabbing hold of her friend's arm in a gesture to get the heck out of there.

"Whatever do you think you are doing!" Allie murmured between clenched teeth as she pulled Nora to the van. They were both giggling like school girls.

"So, wasn't that fun, my friend?" Nora asked.

"Right! Kind of like slitting my wrist!" Allie chuckled.

A flat tire! Oh great!

Just as Nora started dialing for AAA, a young blond man with beautiful blue eyes and a battered hat covering his brow approached them and offered to change their tire.

They accepted his offer intending to pay him for his generosity. He tipped his hat cordially and went about his work without speaking another word. As they were looking in their purses to find some bills, they found the man had disappeared as quickly as he had appeared.

Parked toward the end of the main drive behind some trees, Allie caught site of a white car with a vanity plate on the front. Could that have been Maria? Could she have been the one to flatten their tire? That would not surprise either of them.

Nora picked up speed and raced down the drive and onto the dirt road leading back to Whispering Heights. As they approached Meadow Way, they spotted the young man who had helped them. He was walking along the road ahead. Nora pulled over to offer him a ride but he disappeared before their eyes.

"Trip?" Allie asked.

"He is watching out for us," Nora responded.

The ghost can take on many guises, they realized.

Two days later, the Southern Sun published an article about a house of ill repute in Ponce de Leon. This was discovered when a well-known city official was seen coming out of what had been dubbed the "pleasure house". A reporter had received a tip, staked himself out at the far end of the parking lot and followed him home. It was then that the man's wife learned about his extracurricular activities. After leaving their house in a rampage, she drove to the so-called pleasure house and confronted Maria about her husband. Denying the accusations, and in a drunken fit of rage, Maria slapped the wife, leaving a visible bruise on her face. The wife filed charges and Maria was arrested and held for several hours until Lucky posted her bail. The city official and the Caluccis were being investigated.

Back at the Inn, Nora and Allie sat in the conservatory among the fragrant miniature orange trees and thought what to do next. Allie felt any quest for revenge was behind her. After all, Maria was in trouble! So Allie convinced Nora they should not continue these kinds of antics as it could damage the reputation of Three Graces.

The following Thursday the newspaper gave several details into the investigation of Maria and Lucky Calluci's house. A storage box had been found under one of the floor boards. Inside was over $100,000 in cash and a book containing names and contact information.

Maybe Detective Holmes would give them more information.

At the police station, Nora and Allie sat waiting over an hour for Holmes.

As she sat checking her e-mail, Nora had noticed a distinguished looking man in one of the offices glancing at them several times as he sat tidying up his desk. *Just like a cop* she thought. *Eagle eyes. They don't miss a trick.* "Frank Matthew Smith, Chief of Police" read the plaque on his door.

"Can I help you with something?" he asked as he closed and locked the door behind him.

"Oh, thank you," Nora replied, "but we are waiting to see Detective Holmes."

"Well you might have a little wait. He just called that he got delayed, but should be here in about half an hour. Can you wait?"

"Yes, thank you."

"I'm Frank Smith, by the way."

Nora shot a glance at the nameplate on his office door, tilted her head and raised an eyebrow. "Yes," she smiled. "I gathered. I'm Nora Donnelly."

"Allie McAllister." Allie extended her hand.

"Pleased to meet you, ladies. I was just on my way out to the canteen for a coffee to go. Can I get you something?"

"Do they have hot chocolate in this canteen of yours?" Nora asked. "I think I'm getting a sugar low."

"I think so. I'll check but maybe a chocolate bar might bring you up faster," he laughed.

"Allie? How about you?"

"I'd really appreciate a black coffee if you don't mind."

About five minutes later, he was walking toward them with a cardboard tray containing two coffees, a hot chocolate and a chocolate bar.

It was 5:30 when Detective Holmes arrived. They spoke to him about Maria's interest in the dresser but omitted their little escapade involving the slashed tire. Though he was already investigating the connection between the Calucci family and the missing girl, Holmes was very interested to hear what they had to say. He was particularly intrigued to hear confirmation of the timing between Tony Calluci being in the Balemas, when the dresser was sold and the time Kalyani Bowers was reported missing.

He confirmed there were charges against Maria for assault and she and her husband were being charged with operating a house of prostitution. The Paradise B&B

had been shut down and the Callucis' cars confiscated that morning.

Nora finally admitted the incident at the B&B, stating she felt the tire had been slashed by someone. Allie added she saw a parked car resembling Maria's on their way out of the B&B.

Detective Holmes confided the trunk of Maria's car contained several bricks as well as a knife with melted rubber stuck to it. He said the rubber resembled the type tires are made of.

So, it was Maria who had thrown the brick into their window...and it was Maria who had slashed their tire, they realized.

They asked again about the missing Indian girl. He only said the matter was under investigation. He was sorry but couldn't elaborate any further.

What he also didn't tell them was an undercover cop had been assigned to the B&B two weeks ago, possibly the man the two women saw when they were there.

"I'll bet that little black book is interesting," Nora said smiling wildly at the detective.

As it turned out, a clergyman, a law enforcement officer, a politician and a number of others were listed in that book and they too were being questioned.

There are going to be a lot of unhappy wives when this all comes out, they thought.

Allie invited Sean for dinner on Tuesday. Caitlin was the norm at dinnertime and Nora also invited Mike. Concerned, Allie consulted Cook after the fact but her response was, "Oh, yes, Mum! I have made plenty of beef stew so there's enough for everyone." She frequently made extra in case someone wanted a hot lunch the following day.

It was 6 o'clock when Sean arrived, handsomely dressed in a short-sleeved white Columbia shirt, khaki cargo shorts and brown Birkenstock sandals.

Allie had taken extra time to apply some light makeup and her hair had been cut in a sassy bob. She wore a chartreuse sundress with small pink flowers embroidered along the neckline and hem and wore pink sandals, showing off her freshly polished toes.

Caitlin was surprised when her mother escorted Sean into the kitchen. "How nice to see you again, Sean." And she was more than delighted to see Mike there.

As they sat around the table and talked, exchanging stories about their work and lives, Sean told them about his wife having suffered for so long with cancer and finally succumbing a few years before. He was thankful for his work and the acquaintances he had made and was happy with the cottage he had built at Casey Key after she passed. He explained he couldn't live in the house they had purchased when she became ill because it held too many sad memories.

Though Allie had already heard the story, she was touched by his sensitivity. *How sad for him and his family.*

The staff at the Inn got so large that it was important to have weekly Wednesday staff meetings.

Tammy Smith, a young single mother, was hired as the Inn's Personal Assistant, working on Monday, Wednesday and Friday mornings while her daughter was in day-care. She also occasionally came in other mornings to help with the phones and bookkeeping. Most of the correspondence, which either Nora or Allie dictated into a recorder, was typed from Tammy's home. They liked the idea of being able to accommodate a young mother's schedule.

Everything was typed on Inn stationery which displayed the Three Graces logo and contact information. All guest reservations were confirmed by mail when appropriate, thank you notes with an invitation to return were mailed after guest stays and newsletters listing upcoming events were e-mailed to their contacts quarterly. All led to a great following through repeat guests and word-of-mouth advertising.

XI. The "Escape"

Cottage construction began in early January and the crew arrived at dawn to begin excavating the grounds for the first cottage. Caitlin and Mike, both in overalls and hard hats, were on the scene to supervise. Mike had brought in his builders as well as subcontractors for pool and shuffleboard court construction. Other workers came in to prepare the canal waterfront and build a small boat launch.

Walkways connected to those at the Inn, leading guests around the property, the gardens and canal where a footbridge to the Clubhouse had already been constructed.

Everyone was enthusiastic and, with Mike's gentle yet strong nature, only five months into construction, the Cottages and grounds were nearly complete.

Mike and Caitlin seemed to enjoy working together and Nora and Allie enjoyed seeing the interaction between the two.

Only one glitch...It was two months into construction when one of the cottages collapsed, apparently for no reason.

Was this perhaps too much activity for Trip to handle?

Mike invited Dr. Douglas, Don Cypress and Sean to take a look. As Don circled the property, he said, "I don't see anything unusual except that this particular building seems to be very close to some graves." He was pointing toward the Crocker graves. "I don't know if you believe in this sort of thing," he said looking at Mike, "but you might be a little **too** close."

"I guess that might be possible," Mike reluctantly admitted.

"I think we should move this particular cottage to the other side of the property," Caitlin said. "After all, Trip deserves to rest in peace with his family."

Nora and Allie agreed. So, the collapsed frame was picked up, the ground leveled off, and plans were made to turn that area of the property into a park-like setting with wild flowers for bird and butterfly watching.

Allie had read in a news article that Maria's father, a man by the name of Jon Thorpe, was the owner of Pirates Cove Inn, a very respectable establishment located on the Peace River in Lacadia. Oddly enough, the next

Southwest Florida Innkeepers' meeting was to be held at his inn the following week.

After the Innkeepers' meeting, Allie and Nora introduced themselves to Jon and asked they could meet with him for a few minutes. Jon invited them to join him for a drink at the Inn's Fog Horn Bar. Both ladies ordered tea lattes. He ordered a double Scotch.

They talked a bit about the meeting as well as the developments at the Three Graces. It was very cordial until Allie mentioned she knew Maria. "You see, Maria married my ex-husband, Daniel but now they are divorced. That's how I know her. I understand she now goes by the name Calucci.

"If you're trying to get at that newspaper article, I want to make perfectly clear I take no responsibility for my daughter's shenanigans!" he emphasized in a low but stern tone. "What she has done or what she continues to do has nothing to do with me."

"I am so very sorry, Mr. Thorpe. We really do not mean to intrude or upset you. But, since we were here today, I just wanted to meet you and to offer my condolences about the situation. Maria seems to be a very troubled woman and I feel badly for her. I just wanted you to know."

Jon ordered the bartender to bring him another Scotch as the first seemed to vanish rapidly. "I'm sorry too. I have never been able to help her and now I refuse. She's gotten mixed up with a bunch of thugs; and, to tell you the truth, after the last article in the paper when they associated me and my inn with her, I'm concerned my business will suffer because of all this publicity."

Nora was quiet but Allie continued, "Let me assure you, Mr. Thorpe, we hope all good things for you and your inn and it would please us to bring your brochures to Three Graces to share with guests who might want to stay in your area."

He relaxed a bit and thought *I wish my daughter were more like this young woman.*

Maria's rented candy apple red vehicle wove up the driveway and came to a screeching halt. Caitlin and Mike spotted her as they were walking to the Inn for lunch. Out of the car she stumbled, her short, tight dress twisted and her wide-brimmed hat askew. Caitlin rushed to the side door to warn her mother and Mike went to the car in an attempt to keep her at bay. As Allie opened the front door and stepped onto the veranda, she spotted Maria's unstockinged legs and spike heels wavering up the steps. Mike had been unable to keep her at the car. Nora and

Allie had taken out a restraining order against Maria so Caitlin called the police.

"Yes, Maria? What are you doing here?"

"I thought I'd pay you little a visit. Why are you snooping around my B&B? You don't have any reason to go to my house. I don't want you there, so STAY AWAY," she yelled. "The cops are asking where I was when you came to the house. They asked me about some stuff they found in my car. Are you trying to pin something on me?"

"Maria, please keep your voice down. I have guests."

"I don't care about your @#%&ing guests," she snarled.

"Shhh," Allie tried to quiet her. "Maria, please understand I am not accusing you of anything. We have had some incidences; and, for some reason, the police seem to think you may have been involved. That's all. I mean you no harm."

Maria got closer and Allie smelled the liquor, noticing she was more than a bit disheveled, her red lipstick smeared over her front teeth and her sunglasses tilted crookedly on her nose. She slurred, "See, I've got a lot more money than you and I can do anything I want! I will take you out if it's the last thing I do!"

Taken aback by the threat, Allie chose to ignore it saying, "Daniel didn't have that much money, Maria. How did you become so wealthy?"

"HA!" Maria snorted. I married myself a Sugar Daddy. Daniel didn't give me much of anything and wouldn't on his dying bed, either. Wanted to make sure his perfect, precious little daughter got his inheritance. Bastard!

"I really won the jackpot with Mr. Lucky Calucci, though. Ugly as sin, but is he ever loaded! And he knows how to treat a lady! Buys me anything I want!"

"Is that your married name, Calucci?"

"Yeh, what's it to you?"

"Well, I met your father and his last name is Thorpe. Thorpe must be your birth name," Allie responded but didn't get an answer.

Maria was swaying and Allie did not want to have her guests see this woman. She took Maria by the arm and escorted her to her car. Maria wriggled herself into the seat indignantly and Allie slammed the door shut. Through the open window, she cheerfully said, "Thank you for stopping by. Drive carefully." At that, Maria revved the engine and peeled around the circular drive and out to the main road, knocking down a flower pot and a few garden lights on her way.

The police were waiting for her as she approached the lane.

Her "Sugar Daddy" showed up at the station and bailed her out.

Lucky had followed his father's footsteps and was also known to the police as a member of the mob but they hadn't been able to prove anything, until now. As was his deceased father being the suspected killer of Kalyani Bowers, Lucky was being investigated into her abduction and torture.

Her day staff had left and Suzanne was finishing her evening work, testing equipment and waiting for the evening staff to arrive. She then, as usual, would inform them as to incoming and outgoing flight traffic for the night. For now, everything was quiet.

As she waited for their arrival, she sat back and put her feet up on the desk, having full view of the setting sun over the calm runways. She had talked to Drew earlier in the day about their plans for Saturday night and dialed the phone. "Allie, it's me."

"Oh, hi, Suzanne! I've been thinking of you, meaning to call."

"Yes, it's been a while so wanted to let you know Drew and I have Saturday off and were wondering if y'all might like to come over for a BBQ and a few beers. I can't remember when we've both had the same day off...it seems like months!"

"I'd love to, Suzanne. Let me check with the rest...." and then she heard Suzanne shout.

"Oh, WAIT a minute! Oh my God! Two people are boarding Winston Chase's plane! There's been no clearance!" She hung up the phone and called Drew who in turn called the police.

What? Allie wondered.

Drew called later that evening,. He had finished with the police and was waiting for Suzanne to phone in to her supervisor. It appeared Suzanne had recognized the woman boarding the plane as the same woman she had encountered in the pit bull incident - Maria Calucci. All the necessary reports had been made to the police who had both Maria and Lucky in custody. They were seized with over two million dollars in cash. It appeared they intended to hijack the plane and flee the country.

Later, Nora and Allie stopped to see Detective Holmes. "The day Maria came to the Inn and wanted us to give her the dresser, she said it had belonged to her in-laws and one of the sons sold it to Big Jim when they were traveling in the Balemas. Do you think they had taken the girl with them?"

While Detective Holmes was more than happy to get this information, he was not pleased the two women were making a good attempt at trying to solve the case themselves. "Thank you, Ladies," and he stood up to show them to the door. Appreciate all your time. I'll be in touch."

Inn of Three Graces   *Lazzeri & Doyle*

XII. One of Many Weddings

Beneath the Live Oaks where life was serene,
Stood a cottage filled with beautiful dreams.
The groom stood ready; family views awake.
His wife-to-be gracefully quivered, quaked.

Never was there a more beautiful bride.
Glorious elegance, hope flamed inside.
Promises vowed; sweet cottage in the woods.
Fragrantly flowered with blooming dogwoods.

Imagined tomorrows began, arrayed.
Celebrating their future love portrayed.
Together, down life's road they were heading.
Forever won at their cottage wedding.

- Dane Ann Smith-Johnson -

Nora had a phone call from Chief Frank Smith who invited her to dinner. Surprised yet pleased, she accepted.

It was a short drive to Voyagers' Village and he had reserved a table overlooking the Harbor.

After a wonderful meal of shitake mushroom bisque and Chilean sea bass, they lingered over the remaining bottle of Chablis and talked until nearly eleven o'clock.

Frank, divorced for 17 years, had two adult children. A year apart in age, the two girls graduated from the

Southwestern Connecticut University and were now living in Maryland farming a piece of land they called Green Thumb. "Green Thumb supplies vegetables and dairy products to area restaurants," he said.

He talked about their most famous client being a well-known author and operating an Inn located in the Citcin Mountains called Words that Linger. Having lived in that area of the country and having an Inn of her own, Nora was intrigued. He told her, because an author owned it, there were a number of literary events for the community and nearby Washington had several bus tours there that included brunch and literacy lectures.

Frank Smith did not hesitate to tell her he would take her there some day and Nora was immediately becoming enamored with the Whispering Heights Chief of Police.

Frank's daughters were coming for a visit the following month and she and Frank planned for them to visit the Three Graces and perhaps stay for dinner.

Betsy and Brianna were lovely young women and both engaged to be married. They talked to their father about a double wedding in Florida so he approached Nora and Allie about having it on the Inn's grounds. They never had a wedding there before but agreed, anxious to give it a go. And, now that the Cottages were finished, they would have extra space and accommodations.

The girls met with Nora, Allie and Caitlin. Caitlin started her story board with names of the brides and grooms, the parents and the attendants. They discussed invitations, flowers, a baker and photographer. Caitlin suggested a catered reception on the grounds, depending on the number of guests, or the possibility of holding the reception at the country club.

Fortunately, there was plenty of time as the wedding date was 18 months away, an October wedding. Nonetheless, the time would go quickly.

Nora suggested the girls visit Steven's Bridal when they got back to Maryland and thought bridesmaids might consider dresses of white bodices with brocaded fall flowers and tulip hem skirts. Both girls wanted to carry baskets of fall flowers.

The wedding plan caught the attention of the Whispering Heights radio station and, since it was the Inn's very first wedding, they invited Caitlin for an interview. Caitlin noted all the local enthusiasm and explained what the Inn did in planning the wedding. She went on to describe Three Graces in detail and even talked about its friendly resident ghost. What she didn't know was that someone important was listening.

Lynn Malloy-O'Connor was driving from Calusa to Pyakkahachee when she picked up the 97.5 FM on her car radio. She heard the interview with Caitlin and immediately turned her car around at the next exit. Heading toward the Inn of Three Graces. She stopped for lunch, called the Inn and scheduled an appointment with Caitlin McInerney for the following morning. Caitlin had no idea what this woman might want to speak with her about.

At 9 o'clock, Lynn arrived at the Inn in a smartly tailored yellow suit with bone shoes and a tasteful floral briefcase. Lynn owned three bridal shops in the northeast and was in Florida with the hope of expanding to the Southwest coast.

"Hello Ms. O'Connor," Caitlin greeted, looking every bit as polished as Lynn but decidedly Floridian in her daintily-flowered dress and pink open-toed pumps.

"Please have a seat," as she showed her into the conservatory. Can I offer you something? Coffee, tea, lemonade?"

"Nothing for me, thank you," she responded, settling into a settee near the coffee table where she carefully placed her briefcase.

Caitlin sat next to her.

"Caitlin, thank you for having me on such short notice. I had previously done some market research on Whispering Heights and thought it might be a potential location for one of my businesses. Unfortunately, somehow, I missed learning about Inn of Three Graces until I heard the radio interview yesterday. Since you seem to be very good at wedding planning, I think you might be interested in hearing what I have to say."

She opened her briefcase and pulled out a portfolio. "So, I understand the Inn and its beautiful grounds are quite expansive and that you now have recently opened guest cottages and other amenities, as well as having a partnership with Whispering Moss Country Club. I would actually love a tour when we're finished speaking if you don't mind and have the time."

"Of course," Caitlin responded. "We're always happy to show off what we've accomplished here. But I'm curious to hear why you've come."

"That's what I prefer! Someone who gets to the point!" She smiled.

"So, I want to propose you consider opening a bridal business on the Inn's property. Through Brides, Inc., your business would be fully stocked with gowns which I would supply. That would include bridal, attendants, mothers' and all accessories. And, since you don't have a tuxedo rental shop nearby, the groom would not be forgotten. This would be a turnkey shop, where brides could plan the ceremony and reception, order invitations, flowers, live music and even favors and place cards. We would also negotiate with a local restaurant for receptions if you don't have the space here. The wedding ceremony could be held right here or at a local church, synagogue, park, beach, or any other venue, for that matter. That too would be arranged by your shop. It would be a turn-key operation and my associates would work with you every step of the way."

Caitlin was wonderstruck over this prospective new venture and took the portfolio Lynn was handing her. "This really does sound like an exciting opportunity, Lynn. I will definitely meet with my mother and her partner about this and will call you."

After a complete tour of the property in a golf cart which Caitlin expertly maneuvered, she asked, "When do you expect to be back to your office?"

"Later next week. But please do give me a ring on my cell if you want to chat." At that, she drove off in her rented Mercedes convertible and waved as she turned onto the main road.

Caitlin sent a text to Allie, Nora and Mike to meet her for lunch where she told them about Lynn Malloy-O'Connor's proposal. They all looked at each other, Nora and Allie shaking their heads in pleasant disbelief, smiling warmly over the idea.

"This sounds like an incredibly fabulous opportunity! The brides wouldn't have to leave the premises, not even to shop for gowns," Allie said.

"Where would we put the shop? What about additional parking? Would we need another entrance drive? Who would we have staff the shop?" Nora was full of questions.

"Let's ask Trip!" Allie joked. Nora nodded with a wide smile.

They never did get around to the Ouija board but Trip showed signs of approval with a double rainbow the following morning. Just to be on the safe side, though, they decided to open Three Graces Bridal Shop off site. A small parcel of land adjacent to Whispering Moss was available and they would place an offer on it.

After all, there was just so much a ghost could tolerate.

Eleanor Parker was hired as their Bridal Consultant and Seamstress and Nora's daughter and her fiancé, who had moved to a small community just outside Whispering Heights, were to manage the business and liaise with Brides, Inc.

The first clients to come to the newly opened shop, of course, were Brianna and Betsy along with their fiancés and Frank and his ex-wife who were paying for the affair.

Nora thought that meeting might be awkward but it was very pleasant. Frank's ex-wife had a new life with her now husband and Frank had no animosity, being content with the way things were and that they were all able to participate in this very important day of their daughters' lives.

Gowns had been purchased in Maryland while the new shop was being built and Caitlin had already ordered and received the invitations. Now they needed to discuss a few last-minute details and arrange for honeymoon packages.

Four days later, Kristin and Laurence made an appointment; and two days after that, Mark and Athena. It appeared they were already off to a fast rolling start with their new venture.

It was October 15th, the day of Brianna and Betsy's weddings. The ceremony was beautifully done, bride and groom and witnesses to the left and right under the pergola before the Three Graces fountain. Dinner was served under the oak hammock and a platform had been laid for dancing.

Mike smiled at Caitlin. "May I have this dance?" And offered his hand in chivalry. They were playing *Always and Forever* by Rod Temperton.

She smiled back, took his hand and they walked out onto the dance floor.

Always and forever
Each moment with you is just like a dream to me
That somehow came true
And I know tomorrow will still be the same
'Cause we've got a life of love that won't ever change

The tempo changed and he twirled her. She laughed and he smiled.

Everyday love me your own special way
Melt all my heart away with a smile
Take time to tell me you really care
And we'll share tomorrow together
I'll always love you
Forever, forever

He drew her closer again.

There'll always be sunshine when I look at you
Something I can't explain just the things that you do
And if you get lonely phone me
And take a second to give to me that magic you make

He whispered in her ear, "I will love you always and forever, Caitlin," and kissed her softly on the lips. "Can the next wedding at Three Graces be ours?"

She smiled widely and winked her eye. "Maybe after Kristin and Lawrence. And then after Mark and Athena. After all, they spoke up first," she laughed.

He kissed her finger and touched it to his lips.

"OK, then," he smiled reaching into his breast pocket, "will you hold onto this and let me know when you're not too busy planning other peoples' weddings?"

A ring!

Nora and Frank were dancing and Allie and Sean were watching the four of them. Sean reached for Allie's hand and smiled at her.

~

The luminous glows of Trip, Hachi and Baby Edward were visible beside the palmettos, Trip smiling and holding a battered hat to his heart.

I'm Cheryl Doyle and I'm Carol Lazzeri

and we've co-authored Inn of Three Graces.

One might ask, "What gave you the idea and how did you manage to write it as a team?"

Well, one day over lunch, we started bantering about how nice it would be to have a beautiful inn in North Port. North Port is growing by leaps and bounds; and, not only does it currently have no hotels, but it also does not have an inn where people can go to fully enjoy an old Florida setting along with its accompanying peace and tranquility. So, we decided to put our inn on paper, creating a town much like North Port called Whispering Heights and calling the story *Inn of Three Graces*, in honor of North Port's historic monument, a sculpture of three dancing ladies in a fountain.

So, "How did we write the book as a team and still remain friends?" one might ask.

It was actually quite an interesting journey. We did have an initial one-on-one meeting and a few along the way; but most of the ideas and writing were sent to each other electronically. It was fascinating the way things evolved. Much like the TV program *Who's Line Is It*, one of us would write a few lines, a few paragraphs or a few pages, always leaving an unfinished idea. After e-mailing it on to our respective co-author, she would pick up the thought and run with it. Sometimes, this was a tough thing to do. One such time was when a wig was found in a dresser which was being held in storage. "What on earth am I going to do with this crazy insert and what's the purpose of bringing a wig, of all things, into this story?" Well, after some thought, the wig is actually found to be a human scalp which puts an unanticipated turn of events into the story. The entire process was an intriguing adventure with many twists and turns. The main thing is that it was fun and that it will be fun for our readers!

The book is written for all to enjoy, with the hope the proverbial bug will catch someone's ear, latching onto our idea and actually accomplishing in reality what we have put on paper - building a beautiful inn in our Wonderful City!

Our readers will find *Inn of Three Graces* to be a lovely story of two friends, Nora and Allie, who set out to build an Inn in Southwest Florida's fictional Whispering Heights community.

We hope you enjoy your journey through this book as enjoyable as we did!

Inn of Three Graces
~ *a tale of adventure, intrigue and comedy* ~

Made in the USA
Columbia, SC
04 June 2018